WORSER

WORSER

JENNIFER ZIEGLER

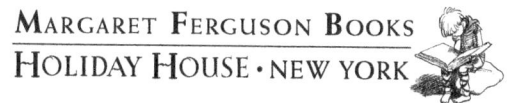

MARGARET FERGUSON BOOKS
HOLIDAY HOUSE · NEW YORK

Margaret Ferguson Books
Copyright © 2022 by Jennifer Ziegler
All Rights Reserved

HOLIDAY HOUSE is registered in the U.S. Patent and Trademark Office.
Printed and bound in March 2023 at Maple Press, York, PA, USA.
www.holidayhouse.com
First Hardcover Edition, 2022 | First Paperback Edition, 2023
3 5 7 9 10 8 6 4

Library of Congress Cataloging-in-Publication Data

Names: Ziegler, Jennifer, 1967– author.
Title: Worser / by Jennifer Ziegler.
Description: First edition. | New York : Holiday House, [2022] | Audience: Ages 10 to 12. | Audience: Grades 4-6. | Summary: William Wyatt Orser's life is turned upside down after his mother has a stroke, but the socially awkward, word-loving twelve-year-old finds glimmers of hope when he discovers friends who share his love of wordplay and books.
Identifiers: LCCN 2021013007 | ISBN 9780823449569 (hardcover)
Subjects: CYAC: Change—Fiction. | Vocabulary—Fiction. | Plays on words—Fiction. | Cerebrovascular disease—Fiction. | Aunts—Fiction. Mothers—Fiction. | Friendship—Fiction. | Bookstores—Fiction. Middle schools—Fiction. | Schools—Fiction. | LCGFT: Novels.
Classification: LCC PZ7.Z4945 Wo 2022 | DDC [Fic]—dc23
LC record available at https://lccn.loc.gov/2021013007

ISBN: 978-0-8234-4956-9 (hardcover)
ISBN: 974-0-8234-5456-3 (paperback)

for Erica Eynouf

Contents

one: Rally 1
two: Bear 11
three: Outlet 25
four: Accommodations 33
five: Occupation 48
six: Courtesy 57
seven: Appeal 73
eight: Revealing 81
nine: Reflection 97
ten: Trip 110
eleven: Perfect 123
twelve: Belongings 136
thirteen: Offense 155
fourteen: Patronize 170
fifteen: Representation 178
sixteen: Admission 190
seventeen: Storm 201
eighteen: Loss 213
nineteen: Limbo 224
twenty: Restore 236
Acknowledgments 245

WORSER

ONE

Rally

"I understand that you had quite a difficult summer, Will."

Worser remained still and silent, refusing to even blink. Principal Ludlum knew nothing about him, no matter what the official records showed. For one thing, Mr. Ludlum kept referring to him as Will. No one called him that. To his mother and his teachers, he was William. He was called Worser by everyone else in school—including, once, accidentally (he hoped), the school secretary.

Mr. Ludlum appeared to be what Worser's mother called a *standoffishial*—one of those administrators who hides in an office all day avoiding people. It was Mr. Vaccario, the assistant principal, who was the perceived figure of authority. He was the one who stalked the hallways of Oak Valley Middle School threatening students and had a face that was rough and red like a meatball.

Throughout sixth grade, Worser had rarely seen Mr. Ludlum. And he'd certainly never been in his office, not until ten minutes ago, at the end of his first week of seventh grade.

And Worser was not impressed.

Mr. Ludlum's stooped posture, rumpled suit, and unchanging expression of surprise-bordering-on-panic—as if he couldn't remember how he came to be in his current location—didn't exactly inspire fear. To believe that the title of *principal* gave him instant authority would be like believing a uniform gave a Boy Scout the ability to lead troops into battle.

"You probably think that what you did wasn't that bad. You probably think that because the school year has only just begun, we are going easy on offenders. You probably think that because you are an honor student"—the principal lifted the file that lay open on the table in front of him, making its sides flap like wings—"we won't take any serious action."

Worser waited for the eventual thesis statement. For all their talk about productivity, educators were some of the worst time-wasters on the planet. Being the son of a university professor—two when his father was alive—Worser knew that better than most.

"But," the principal continued, "I'm afraid that's *not* how the system works."

There it was. The main point—although not clearly stated. He'd padded it with the phrase *I'm afraid*. Then again, Mr. Ludlum looked a little afraid, so perhaps he accidentally let slip his true feelings. He also used the word *system* instead of *school*. This made Worser imagine himself and all the other students passing through a giant digestive tract toward the inevitable end. The metaphor, he decided, was apt.

"Will?" Principal Ludlum's voice lowered and took on weight—the same weight it had when he announced disaster drills over the intercom. "Why will you not answer me?"

Worser lifted his left eyebrow. "Because you haven't asked me any questions. You have used only declarative sentences."

The principal's expression grew slightly more startled. He made a few random vowel sounds before clearing his throat. "Do you know why you were sent in here this afternoon?"

"Yes."

Worser's brief reply seemed to disappoint the principal. "Perhaps you would like to explain your misbehavior in your own words," he said with a sigh, his back sliding a couple of inches down his office chair.

"I was in the library reading, and apparently that went against school policy."

Principal Ludlum took off his glasses and rubbed the space between his brows. "It was not that you were reading. That was not the problem, was it? The problem was that you were supposed to be somewhere else. Do you remember where we asked all students to be at three o'clock, per today's special schedule?"

Worser disliked this practice of asking obvious questions. It served no real purpose and succeeded only in making people feel like kindergartners.

"Yes," he replied. "Students were asked to report to the gymnasium at three o'clock. I felt that reading would be a better use of my time than watching cheerleaders spell *Oak Valley* with their bodies. I already know how to spell both *oak* and *valley*, as well as many other words."

"There is no reason to be snide, young man."

"I'm merely frustrated. I would think that in this age of video games and cell phones that school administrators would reward a student who wanted to read or write—not send him to the office."

Again, the principal let out a series of incomprehensible sounds before deflating with a long sigh. "You appear to be...good with words," he said. "Do you know what *rally* means?"

Worser, who had been occupying the chair across from Mr. Ludlum like a jellyfish in a teacup, suddenly leaned forward and elongated. He forgot his plan to be as unmoving and close-mouthed as possible.

"*Rally*," Worser began. "I suspect you are referring to the noun form of the word, which means 'a gathering of people with a common interest.'"

"Correct. Today we held a pep rally, a gathering designed to boost pride in one's school community. I think you would agree that a sense of unity among you and your peers is important—at least as important as the words in the book you were reading."

Worser's hand clenched. "My peers? The same people who have teased me and kicked my backpack to the rear of the bus so often that I've decided to walk to and from school instead? The same people who delight in placing vile things on my chair and referring to me by a hateful and ungrammatical nickname? Do I think that a sense of unity with *them* is equal in value to words? No, I do not. Words elevate our species. They are the basis of civilized society. There is nothing more important than words."

Worser knew this was the wrong answer, but he didn't care. He would much rather report to in-school detention and sit between two future armed robbers than say that a school pep rally was worth as much as the written word. Principal Ludlum might not have realized it, but his question went right for Worser's jugular. Worser had to defend himself.

The principal studied Worser, and Worser studied the

principal, waiting for the verdict. Would Mr. Ludlum dole out the sentence himself or call in that thug of an assistant principal? He hoped it wouldn't come to that. Not that he feared Mr. Vaccario's sweaty, vein-popping rants. He'd just had enough of school for one day and was eager to get home and work on more important things.

"Well—" Mr. Ludlum began in his lackluster voice. But he never got to complete his sentence, because right then the door opened, and a woman dressed from head to toe in purple stepped into the office.

"There you are, Potato," the woman said to Worser.

The school secretary's apologetic face peered around the doorframe. "Excuse the interruption, Mr. Ludlum. The boy's mother is here."

Worser winced. "She's *not* my mother."

Worser sat in the passenger seat of Aunt Iris's rattly, lima-bean-colored Volkswagen Squareback. Every bump bounced him hard enough to strain against his seat belt and was accompanied by a high-pitched, almost rodent-like squeak from somewhere in the machinery—but he didn't mind. His detainment in the school office had been demoralizing and pointless, and the ride was an assault on his senses, but at least he'd been spared the walk home.

"My, my," Aunt Iris kept repeating. She also appeared to be shaking her head, but that could have been due to the jostling motions of the car. After a half dozen *mys*, she regarded him with a saintly smile and said, "Well now, I suppose there's no good reason to tell your mom about your little disturbance, especially since that nice principal decided not to discipline you."

Before they'd left the office, Mr. Ludlum explained that he felt his "stern talking-to" was punishment enough and that—in a reversal of his earlier statement—he could be lenient because Worser was an honor student.

"But you are lucky Ms. Lucretia was home and able to sit with her. I really don't like leaving your mom in the care of others—even for just a little while. So no more monkeyshines, okay?"

Worser replied with a sound like *mmm*.

"Your mom is having such a terrific day, and I don't want to ruin it. She did wonderfully at her therapies, ate lots of lentil soup for lunch, and took a nice nap. It has definitely been a purple day. Deep and serene. Isn't that wonderful?"

Worser acknowledged Aunt Iris with a new sound—part sigh and part grunt.

"And she just loves listening to music on the radio. She wants me to keep it on that classical station. She particularly enjoyed that one song that went *ya DA da-da daaaah*...." Aunt Iris continued warbling a melody with nonsense syllables, her right hand letting go of the steering wheel so that she could conduct an invisible orchestra.

"She does not like listening to music," Worser said. "You just think she does."

Aunt Iris was imagining things. His mother had always said music was a waste of time. Silence was her favorite background noise, as it was with him, too. Professor Constance Orser and her late husband, Professor Reginald Orser, twenty years older than she, had never owned a sound system, a television, or a cell phone. They had also, according to his mother, been the last in their respective departments at the university to own and operate a computer—and had only given in due to pressure. Bound books had been their preferred methods of gathering information as well as entertainment.

"Oh, but she does enjoy it," Aunt Iris said. "I know so."

"How? Did she tell you she likes it?"

Aunt Iris stopped singing. "That's a terrible thing to say."

Worser closed his eyes—his best strategy for dealing with Aunt Iris. He was not used to interacting with someone of her nature for extended periods of time. Aunt Iris was emotional, expressive, eager, ebullient. A walking string of *e* modifiers. *Eeeeeeee!* Worser, meanwhile, was bookish and standoffish, and preferred hushed tones—all words with *shhh* appropriately enough. Opposite sounds, opposite personalities.

He supposed he should feel guilty for what he'd said, but he didn't, especially since it rewarded him with silence from his aunt. For the next few minutes, all he heard were the screeches and rumbles of the car. When he opened his eyes again, the Volkswagen was pulling onto the cracked cement driveway next to his mom's Nissan.

Aunt Iris met his gaze. "Please be patient and kind, okay?"

Worser wasn't sure if his aunt wanted him to be patient and kind to her or to his mother, but he nodded.

This seemed to appease her, because she simultaneously switched off the car and switched on her singing. *"Ya DA da-da daaaah..."*

As she and her scarves fluttered up the walkway and through the front door, Worser pretended to fumble with something in his backpack in order to lag behind on the porch—another way of coping. He needed a brief pause—a semicolon, or perhaps an ellipsis—so he could transition. Not from school to home or outside to inside, but from what was to what now is.

He bounced on the loose boards and studied the shadows cast by light straining through the contents of five hanging baskets. Spider plant had begotten spider plant, which had begotten more spider plants—hundreds of the spindly spawn—most of them now shriveled and dead from the Texas heat, creating a thatched curtain over the porch front. Aunt Iris often bemoaned that they were probably beyond saving, and that she'd one day get rid of the poor carcasses. But Worser hoped not. He actually liked the cover they provided and admired the stubborn way they remained tethered to one another.

"Oh, here he is." Ms. Lucretia, their next-door neighbor, was stepping onto the porch. "We were just wondering what was keeping you."

"You still out there, Potato?" Aunt Iris poked her head around the front door.

Worser was annoyed at being interrupted, annoyed that his aunt would ask about the obvious, and annoyed that she persisted in calling him Potato. He already felt as if he were the only seventh grader in town who hadn't launched into puberty—and being referred to by the nickname she'd given him as a baby didn't help. Then again, as he studied his rounded shadow on the porch floor, he had to admit his short, stout shape did look rather potato-like. Perhaps she couldn't help herself.

Ms. Lucretia crossed her arms. She never smiled—at least at him. Normally, he was fine with that, as he despised it when grown-ups gave condescending smiles. She also didn't give him wide-eyed pitying looks like most of the adults he'd recently interacted with—another plus. She'd been his neighbor his entire life and usually just said things like "Hello" or

"Tell your mother I accepted a package for her" or "Don't you dare step on my flowers." All acceptable in his view. But in that moment, as she stared at him, he felt entirely too seen.

"You should go on in," Ms. Lucretia said as she headed toward her house.

Worser sighed, shouldered his backpack, and stepped through the open front door.

His mother was standing in the foyer, waiting for him. "Be! Be! Be!"

"Hi,... Mom." Worser heard the pause in his greeting and hated himself for it.

He wondered when he would get used to thinking of this person as his mother. It had been three months since the stroke—a bursting blood vessel that laid waste to a section of his mother's brain the same way a bomb could level a town and cut off key supply routes.

Everything about her had changed. She held her head at a new sideways angle, more upturned than before. Her brisk trot had turned into a shamble. Her eyes were wider, her mouth a tilde—higher on her left, slack on her right. The hair she'd always kept in a no-nonsense bob was growing out shaggy and wild, except for a section of very short hair above her left ear where she had been shaved for the operation. And her power of speech was gone.

"Be!" She smiled at him and held up her thin, shaking arms. Dr. Constance Orser, professor of rhetoric, had lost all her words.

Worser had spent his summer waiting in rooms: actual waiting rooms, plus hospital rooms, Aunt Iris's apartment, and the lobby of the rehab facility. First, he waited to learn whether his mother would survive. Next, he waited for her to regain consciousness. After that, he waited for her to be transferred to the rehab facility. Now he waited for her return. She had been back at home for three weeks, but she herself had not come back.

Every morning he expected his mom to talk to him again, to share an interesting tidbit from the *New York Times* or read aloud a laughably incongruous sentence from a student's paper—or even criticize him. But at present all she could manage were random syllables beginning with *b*.

Rally. In verb form it meant to recover, bounce back. Worser's mother had not yet rallied.

TWO

Bear

After a snack of leftover lentil soup and more talk from Aunt Iris about how purple a day it had been, Worser finally made it up to the comfort and privacy of his room. Here there were no distractions. No bright colors, taped whale songs, or strange herbal fragrances. A smell did, in fact, emanate from his room—a sour odor, like lunchmeat a few days past its expiration date. But Worser couldn't detect it anymore, having become desensitized to it over the years.

He reached into his backpack and pulled out a large loose-leaf binder. It was battered and cracked, and the seam in the front was starting to give way. Tucked inside the clear plastic pocket on the cover was a yellowing piece of notebook paper that read, in nine-year-old Worser's careful lettering, *Masterwork by William Wyatt Orser*.

The binder was full—perhaps a bit too full, which contributed to the strain on the cover. Not counting the 17 empty pages in the back, there were 321 pages of writing—all lists of important observations Worser had made over the past three and a half years. Observations about words.

Worser took the pile of folded, freshly laundered shirts

that Aunt Iris had placed on the foot of his bed and transferred them to the floor. He sat on them as he settled into his usual at-home work spot: on the carpet with his back against his bed. As he stared down at the clean blue lines of the paper, he felt the usual quiet excitement—that subtle fizzy sensation surging through his body, concentrating in his fingertips.

He tapped his pen against his lips a few times as his thoughts whirred into a higher, smoother gear. Then he hunched over the notebook and wrote at the top of the page "Word Contradictions." He had Aunt Iris to thank for this latest entry. Their conversation in the car had spurred the idea.

"If *terrific* can mean the opposite of *terrible*, why isn't *horrific* the opposite of *horrible*?" he wrote.

Good. What else? He knew that *flammable* and *inflammable* meant the same thing, even though they looked like opposites. Also, there were other words that seemed as if they should be antonyms but were actually synonyms, like the nouns *caretaker* and *caregiver* and the verbs *bone* and *debone*. *Reckless* sounded as if it meant "disaster-free" when, in fact, it meant "careless and prone to accidents." And *last* could mean, as an adjective, "belonging to the end of something" or, as a verb, "to endure."

Yes, this was a worthy topic for a new entry. As he wrote down his observations, his tongue absently tapped the corners of his mouth, and the lingering annoyance over the events at school and the drive home ebbed away. The sounds of recorded marine animals and Aunt Iris's prattling disintegrated into easy-to-ignore static. He was, finally, alone with his thoughts.

As Worser leaned against his bed and stared up at the

dingy spray-acoustic ceiling, his hands slid backward beneath the bed frame. He was just pondering how *clip* can mean both "to adhere" and "to cut off" when he felt a sharp pain in his left hand.

"Ow!" He glanced under the bed and found Seersucker (Seer for short), one of his aunt's cats, glaring at him. Ears back, pupils like shivs. Worser cupped his throbbing hand in his other and noted four thin red stripes across the knuckles.

For as long as Worser could remember, his bedroom door wouldn't completely shut. Seer had apparently decided to take advantage of this and make himself Worser's antisocial, homicidal roommate. While the other cat, Gingham (Ging for short), was skittish, ghostlike, and rarely seen, Seer always seemed to be lying in wait around corners and under furniture.

Worser scrambled to his feet and opened the door all the way. "Get out, you sadist!" he shouted.

Seer made a demonic noise, part growl, part shriek, that culminated in a fang-bearing hiss before running out of the room—a blur of fluff, stripes, and malevolence.

After making sure there were no other lurking creatures, Worser slammed his door—which, except for the satisfying noise, made no real difference since the door immediately reopened. He then plunked back into his spot and tried to regain that highly charged focus. But it was no use. The fizzy feeling was gone, and so was his concentration.

Grumbling, Worser packed up his Masterwork. He needed to escape to somewhere peaceful, private, and cat-free.

Luckily, he had a place.

Worser had discovered his secret hideout a year ago while searching for a shortcut to middle school. The bus had become unbearable. Loud and jam-packed, full of hurled insults and projectiles—with sixth graders the special targets. Worser couldn't get a seat to himself—no one could—and whoever ended up sitting with him teased him relentlessly. Even the band kids picked on him.

At first, it seemed he had only two alternatives, neither of them appealing. One would involve crossing a terrifying intersection where his neighborhood's main street met the highway, just as it became part of the new tollway. The number of dead skunks, possums, and armadillos at the intersection was a powerful enough warning to prevent him risking it. The second would involve a more tortuous route that would avoid the deadly juncture but require him to get up twenty minutes earlier to allow enough time.

When he consulted a map, Worser noticed a peanut-shaped green space marked MESA SEGURA NATURE PRESERVE that hugged the northern edge of his neighborhood. From the looks of it, if he cut diagonally though the green space, it would lead him to another group of residential streets—one of which led to his school. The entire walk would probably take ten minutes, tops. Determined, he set out to find this route.

The green space turned out to be lovely. It was full of trees—some tall and sturdy, others dark and twisty—that strained the sunlight and muffled the noises of the nearby roads. The ground was cushiony, dotted with occasional rocks, feathery ferns, and big green plants with long, tentacle-like leaves. Unfortunately, the space was also divided lengthwise by a limestone bluff approximately two stories deep, something that hadn't been apparent on the map. Worser had held tight to one of the gnarled trees and peered over the edge. Immediately below, the land was flat and scrubby, with smaller and far fewer trees, and it appeared to be in the process of turning into residential lots, given the coral-colored tape dividing it into rectangles. This open land ended at a road and the neighborhood of split-level, ranch-style homes that led to his school.

He figured there had to be a safe way down. For the next half hour, he searched for a path—to no avail. It was becoming increasingly clear that he'd have to wake up earlier and use the more circular, time-consuming route, as the only way he could use the green space would be via hang glider in one direction and climbing gear in the other.

That's when a miracle had happened.

As Worser leaned defeatedly against a tall red oak, he'd noticed a timeworn piece of wood nailed into the tree. He discovered another roughly twenty inches above it. Then another and another—a set of seven rungs total, all leading up to a wooden platform. Worser, who detested physical activity, including rope climbing in gym class, nonetheless found himself clambering up.

He had no idea how old the tree house was, but it was in good enough shape to make him feel safe. The platform was weather-beaten, yet solid, and only one of the rungs near the top was slightly wiggly. Everything else appeared to be sound. After carefully checking for any exposed nails or hidden hornets' nests, he leaned back against the tree trunk, feeling strangely exhilarated.

And that was when a second miracle happened.

From his perch, he could see over the trees and down the bluff to the road with ranch-style homes, well-kept lawns, and minivans in the driveways. One house, gray brick with creamy white trim and shutters, seemed familiar to him. He couldn't quite place it at first. But not five minutes later, a dark green Volvo pulled up and four people got out. He knew them immediately. A father, mother, daughter, and son. The tree house had provided him with a clear, albeit faraway view of Donya Khoury's residence.

Donya—daughter of Dr. Jasar Khoury, professor of poetry and a colleague of his mother's at the university. Donya—who was basically the same age, in the same grade, and had shared three classes with him in elementary school and Advanced Language Arts with him in sixth grade. Donya—the only person outside his family about whom he spent time thinking. Worser felt it was a coincidence too wondrous to ignore and decided then and there to claim the tree house as his own.

Now, almost a year later, he glanced over at Donya's house, hoping to catch a glimpse of her. He visualized her completing her homework at the dining room table. Or maybe flopped on the sofa with her cell phone cupped in her hands. Or doing whatever it was ordinary twelve-year-old girls did at home after school.

Of course, Donya wasn't ordinary. Donya was a being so extraordinary, he counted himself lucky to regularly inhabit the same building she was in. Eight years earlier, four-and-a-half-year-old Donya had handed four-year-old Worser a doughnut in the break room beside her dad's office and said, "You're smarter than other kids, aren't you?"

"Yes," he'd replied.

From then on, he'd revered her, usually in silence and from a distance, but with the same indescribable urgency that compelled monarch butterflies to migrate to Mexico and drove king salmon thousands of miles upriver.

His feelings hadn't lessened by the time they started

middle school. Worser thought Donya had the most stunning and exquisite face of any human—the way her eyes lit up and her eyebrows pushed against each other while she read; the way she glared at the heavens whenever she observed asinine behavior at school, as if cursing an invisible god for filling her world with such stupidity; the way she never seemed to wear that expression while observing him.

Daylight was dimming, and shadows were stretching. If Worser wanted to use this time to work, he had to put aside all thoughts of Donya. For the next twenty minutes he tried to write about contradictory words and phrases, but he was too fidgety to think straight. He was still mad at Principal Ludlum, and mad at his aunt for fussing over his mom and swirling about his home. Emotions were pesky things that got in the way of the ordered thinking he needed for his Masterwork. Since his mom's stroke, he'd been especially bad at managing them.

Worser had just started ruminating on how *fine* can mean both "high-quality" and "ho-hum," when he heard the steady crunching of dry leaves. Someone was coming. It happened occasionally. Hikers passing by or stopping to check out the view from the top of the bluff. The first few months after he'd discovered his secret place, he worried someone would show up, claim the platform as their own, and order him down. But no one ever did. And no one else ever seemed to see it. The red oak was well hidden among other trees and plants, and the rungs were the same gray shade as the tree trunk. Besides, people so rarely glanced up.

Judging by the sounds, the person was coming closer. Now, in addition to the tramps and snaps, he could hear low grunts. Maybe an animal? A wild boar or mountain lion? He knew the former couldn't climb trees, but he wasn't sure about the latter. He grasped his pen like a knife and waited for the creature to reveal itself.

And then, twelve months since miracles one and two, miracle number three happened. The creature turned out to be Donya, marching through the trees grumbling to herself. He recognized her dark wavy hair against the Day-Glo green hoodie she always wore—even on late-summer days like today.

Worser was so stunned by the sight of her, he let go of the pen he'd been holding as a makeshift weapon. It bounced off Donya's head just as she passed underneath.

"*Ow!*" She frowned up at him.

"Sorry."

"Worser?"

"Hi."

"Is this your pen?"

"It's all right. I have another."

"What are you doing here?"

"Just sitting and writing. I have my algebra homework with me, too."

Donya wandered around the tree, looking it up and down. "I had no idea this was here. Is this your spot?"

"My...spot?"

"Yeah. You know. Your place to get away from it all."

Worser nodded. "Yes, *refuge* is the term I'd use."

Donya knelt and peered over the edge of the steep bluff—an action that made Worser vibrate with worry.

"I used to have a spot," she said, gazing down. "There was an empty field across the street from our house, and I'd go sit under this big pecan tree and clear my mind. But last year they built our new neighbor's house and fenced in the tree. I wish I were under it now."

"You c-can..." Worser's voice shook. He took a breath and restarted. "You're welcome to come up here. I'll share my spot."

She shook her head. "Can't. I'm afraid of heights."

"Actually, that's a misnomer. Fear of heights is really a fear of falling. Just like fear of the dark is a fear of what might be *in* the dark, not the darkness itself."

Donya stood and clapped dirt from her hands. "I should go. It's been a bad day. I really don't feel like talking or getting lectures on word usage."

Worser watched as she crashed through the nearby thicket, the vivid green of her hoodie fading into the celadon-and-olive tones of the surrounding foliage.

He wished he'd thought of something else to say. He could have told her she could keep the pen. He could have complimented her on her fluorescent hoodie. He could have praised her on her correct usage of the verb *to be* in the subjunctive form: *I wish I were under it now.* His comment about fear of heights wasn't meant to be critical; he just wanted people to say what they meant. It wasn't Donya's fault those inaccurate terms had found their way into the lingo.

Worser decided to head home. He'd been in the tree house for an hour and hadn't made any real progress on his Masterwork. The only thing he'd accomplished was to do to Donya what Seer had done to him: Though by accident and without drawing blood (thankfully), he'd driven her away in frustration.

"Beh?"

Worser ignored his mother and turned to a new page in a book titled *Forgotten English*.

"Beh?" his mother said again. She kept shifting against the pillows that propped her up in her hospital bed, her eyes staying on him the whole time. "Beh?"

He realized he should be happy she'd progressed to a new sound—a short *e* syllable rather than her usual long *e*—but it still didn't make sense. Also, her rising pitch made it come off like a question. Regardless, he couldn't understand it and felt it would be best to carry on as if nothing were happening.

"*Thruffing*," he read aloud. "Lincolnshire dialect for 'the whole matter.' *Thruff*—I wonder if that's related to the word *through*? Or perhaps *thorough*?"

Over the years, this was how they'd usually spent their after-dinner hours, reading to each other. His mother would read lists of the most commonly misspelled words or passages from grammar textbooks—grammar being her favorite subject, even if she did say it was a Sisyphean effort to try to teach it to hormonal college students. Etymology was another interest, and Latin, to an extent. She felt that conjugating Latin verbs was a waste of time, but she did want Worser to grasp common roots and see how English sprouted out of them—not unlike the way a thin green runner would shoot from a half-dead spider plant on the porch. In turn, Worser read to her, graduating from picture books to more complicated fare. He liked to try to stump her with rare words and phrases—those that were used only in particular regions or industries, or that had fallen out of favor over the years.

Now their evening reading time was considerably shortened. Instead of taking place in the living room, it took place in the study—which was being used as his mother's bedroom since she couldn't yet handle the stairs. And now it was only

Worser doing the reading, although he still chose the same subject matter.

"*Throttlebottom*," he went on. "A shrewd—"

"Potato?"

Worser glanced up. Aunt Iris's head—all unruly hair, woven earrings, and sheepish grin—was poking into the room.

"What?" he asked.

"I don't think she's enjoying this. Why not read *Alice* to her?" She pointed to a leather-bound edition of *Alice in Wonderland* that had been pulled off the shelf, dusted clean, and set on his mother's nightstand. "She loved hearing me read the first chapter today."

"Nonsense."

"Why do you doubt me?"

"I'm saying that book is full of silly nonsense, not to mention written by a suspected pedophile," he said. "You don't know what she likes."

"I'm her sister. I grew up with her. I can tell when she's happy and when she isn't."

"I'm her son, and I've lived with her my whole life. I know how she feels about Lewis Carroll. The only reason we have that book is that some clueless acquaintance gave it to her years ago."

"*I* gave it to her."

"I rest my case," Worser mumbled.

Aunt Iris's sigh seemed to defy normal lung capacity. "Fine," she said. "Then why not read her a different story?"

"She doesn't like stories. She likes words."

"That doesn't make sense. If someone likes words, they like stories."

Worser squeezed his eyes shut. "You're not like us. You wouldn't understand."

The curl of Aunt Iris's brows showed him he'd hurt her feelings. He tried to enjoy it, ignoring the heaviness that seeped over him like cold mud.

"I refuse to fight," she said. "I truly hope you two enjoy yourselves. Just remember that she had a long day today and that you'll have more time with her tomorrow and Sunday. She'll need to go to sleep soon."

After Aunt Iris closed the door, Worser grumbled, "What a chuffy snollygoster."

"Beh?"

"Sorry you had to witness that. I was only saying—" Glancing up, he noticed his mother had stretched out her hand, reaching for a framed photo on the side table. It was of Worser as a two-year-old, wearing only a diaper and hugging a stuffed bear. His aunt must have had it framed and placed it there. For all her complaining about clutter, she sure brought in a lot of it herself.

A new thought tugged at him.

"Wait. You want the bear? Is that what you're saying? *Beh* means 'bear'?" he asked.

His mother grinned back at him. It was weak and slightly lopsided, but clearly a smile. "Beh," she said again, raising both arms.

"I'll have to go and get it," he said. "I'll be right back."

He set down *Forgotten English* and hurried upstairs to his room.

The bear. Other than the books he had teethed on, ripped, and covered in drool, the bear was his only memorable toy from childhood. He wasn't sure where it had come from, or if it ever had a name, but he dimly recalled carrying it around. Sometime during his grade school years, he'd abandoned it, setting it on top of the high bookcase in his room. Now and then he spotted it as he lay sprawled on his bed, but otherwise he never gave it any thought. Why his mother wanted it was a mystery.

The bear was slumped despondently against an unused Battleship game. The bookcase was tall, and Worser couldn't remember how he'd gotten the bear up there. Maybe his younger self had tossed it several times until it landed.

He fetched a chair from his mother's bedroom, which was now his aunt's bedroom. Standing on the seat and stretching out his arm, he was able to grasp one of the bear's paws between his fingers and pull it down.

By the time he got downstairs, his mother was lying back in apparent sleep. Her face had gone completely slack and her eyes were closed, though her right eye tended to stay open a tiny bit ever since the stroke. His errand had taken too long—and she was exhausted after her triple shot of speech therapy, physical therapy, and occupational therapy that day. He'd have to give it to her tomorrow.

As Worser turned to leave, his shoulder accidentally hit the doorjamb.

"Ow," he muttered.

"Be?"

His mother's eyes were open, watching him. Again, she smiled, and again he focused on the slight tilt and felt guilty.

"Sorry I woke you. I brought him down like you asked." He walked to her side and tucked the bear under her left arm. "See? There he is."

His mom glanced down at the bear then up at Worser again. "Beh?" she said, her voice low and crackly.

"Yes. Bear." He stood there, unsure of what else to do.

She seemed more confused than happy. Then again, he wasn't confident in his ability to read her lately. He decided she was probably just tired and that he should leave so she could sleep.

"Beh?" she said again, her voice a hoarse whisper.

"Yes. I got you the bear. Rest now, Mom." He watched her image slowly disappear as he closed the door—and was ashamed of the relief he felt when it clicked shut.

THREE

Outlet

"Sorry." Herbie spoke with the same matter-of-fact tone he used with everything he said, without even a hint of embarrassment. Worser squinted up at the glowing tube lights in the school's ceiling and blew out his breath as slowly as possible.

It was Monday morning, and he and Herbie Nestor were standing in their usual pre-start-bell spot—a nook in the wall of the student center. It was safer there, away from all the noise and activity taking place at the tables set out in front of them. The nook was also right next to the school's main office, and only the most dedicated and inspired bully would dare pick on someone within clear view of Mr. Vaccario as he stood at attention, arms crossed, frown in place, watching from the window-walled office a few feet away.

This morning, however, Worser was considering venturing out of this zone of safety. Mainly because the nook kept filling with Herbie's farts.

"Dear god, Herbie. You really put the *scent* in *adolescent*."

"Sorry," Herbie said again. "Nanna says I need to gain

weight, so she's started making me these potato-and-egg scrambles in the morning."

Worser didn't respond. He was too busy holding his breath. It was coming time to inhale again, and he wasn't sure if he should use his nose or mouth. Mouth breathing would likely lessen the smell, but would it also be, in a way, like eating the farts?

He chose his nose and regretted it.

"Have you ever noticed how different people's farts sound?" Herbie asked. "Like how, whenever I fart, it sounds like a question, and whenever you fart, it sounds like a statement?"

"No," Worser said, although, because he was holding his breath, it sounded more like *dough*.

"Do you think people's farts could tell us something about their personalities? Take Nanna's farts, for instance. They're just little pops. Kind of meek—like her. Could the two things be related?"

Worser didn't respond because he was still avoiding inhaling.

"Anyway." Herbie made one of his signature shrugs. "Can I just point out that this conversation mirrors the differences in our fart sounds?"

Worser found Herbie's ramblings a little more inane than usual that morning. That plus the polluted air would have been plenty of reason for him to go elsewhere. But he wouldn't. The fact was, he'd grown dependent on Herbie's presence—especially because Herbie was his only friend.

Their alliance began one day in sixth grade when Herbie approached him in the locker room after PE class and complimented Worser's shirt—a faded Calvin and Hobbes tee. This bold move of Herbie's shocked Worser for two reasons. One, because no one ever approached him voluntarily unless it was to harass him and, two, because he was, at the time, *only* wearing the Calvin and Hobbes shirt. He'd been so taken aback that not a single snappy retort had occurred to him and he ended up saying simply "Thanks"—mainly to get Herbie, who kept on standing there awaiting his reply, to move on.

After that incident, Herbie sought out his company at lunch and fell into step with him whenever he spotted him in the hallway. At first, it annoyed Worser that Herbie would assume they were friends when Worser had never asked him to be one. Then again, Worser wasn't exactly sure of the protocol.

As a roly-poly kindergartner, unaccustomed to conversation with anyone under the age of forty, overwhelmed by social situations, and still unskilled at such practices as blowing his nose, Worser had approached kid after kid on the playground during recess to ask each one to be his friend. Every time he was turned down. Sometimes the kids would kick pea gravel at him. The next year, as an equally awkward and boogery first grader, he had tried it again with the same results. By second grade, he'd come to accept his status as a loner. By third grade he preferred it.

Worser quickly discovered that Herbie had fairly interesting tastes in conversation topics—though not including today's. Also, Herbie never challenged any opinion of Worser's. In fact, nearly everything Worser said was approved of and adopted. But mainly, having someone stand beside him and sit with him in the cafeteria brought a sense of belonging at school he hadn't realized he'd been lacking.

Worser had never spent time with Herbie outside of school. What would they have done? Worser preferred doing homework on his own, and he doubted Herbie was the crossword-puzzle type. Plus, his mother would have found Herbie's questions insufferable. There had been a couple of times when Herbie invited him to his house, but Worser had always politely declined. He hadn't even told him what had happened to his mother.

As Worser stood in the nook and contemplated how to attain oxygen, a flash of fluorescent green caught his eye. It was Donya's hoodie—attached to Donya. She was standing in the office talking to Principal Ludlum.

Just the sight of her seemed to lift Worser out of the noxious cloud he was standing in. He no longer worried about respiration. Instead, he focused on her. Her intense expression, her flailing arms. Whatever she was saying, she certainly believed strongly in it. Even Mr. Vaccario broke his sentry stare to glance over at her. It was difficult to tell, but the slight evening of the vice principal's corrugated face seemed to indicate silent approval. Principal Ludlum, on the other hand, kept glancing at the wall clock, as if hoping for the start bell to rescue him.

Donya said something and made one final grand gesture, her wide brown eyes both angry and pleading. Principal Ludlum's shoulders rose and fell in a sigh, and he answered while shaking his head. With one last furious flash of her eyes, Donya turned and stormed out of the office.

As she stomped past Worser and Herbie, she paused and looked at them.

"Hi," Worser said, raising his left hand.

Donya scrunched up her nose, said, "Eww, what smells so

awful?" and continued on her way, cupping her hands over her face as a makeshift gas mask.

Herbie's problem seemed to clear up by the end of the school day when he and Worser had geography together. It was the only class they shared, and the air in the classroom had had its usual stale aroma of old books mixed with nervous sweat and lemon-scented floor cleaner.

"It's a disgrace that they're having us memorize the states again," Worser said as he stalked out of the classroom with Herbie. "We did that in third grade. What a flagrant misuse of time and resources."

Worser took note of his own increased volume. He was, as his aunt would say, "in a state." It then occurred to him to make a pun about being in a state over the states, but he was too indignant for wordplay.

"Yeah. Probably because most students still can't recognize them on a map," Herbie said striding into place beside him. "I kind of like it, though. Have you ever noticed that Montana's west side looks like a sad man? And New York is a munched-on nacho chip?"

Worser had not noticed, yet he knew he would the minute he studied a map again. Herbie was constantly sharing offhand observations that would forever alter Worser's view of reality. Like his comment about electrical outlets resembling two scared faces, one on top of the other. Now, anytime Worser needed to plug something in, he saw a terrified expression and felt rather violent shoving prongs into its eyes and mouth.

Someone passing by let out a sneering laugh. Worser wasn't sure if it was coincidence, or if the person was laughing at what Herbie said—or at the general sight of the two of them.

He tried to imagine how he and Herbie must look to others. More than once, Worser had been made aware of his resemblance to an overgrown baby, with his protruding belly, round cheeks, round nose, and two chins. Herbie, meanwhile, was all thin tall lines, bony angles, and a scribble of curly hair. They were two cartoon styles, a little-known member of the Peanuts gang walking alongside a Ralph Steadman drawing.

"Where are you going?" Herbie asked.

"To the library."

"The school library?"

Considering the school library was a mere ten yards down the corridor and the closest public library was three miles away, Worser figured the answer was apparent. Still, he replied, "Yes."

"You can't. They're locking it up after school now."

Worser stopped in the middle of the hall, causing the current of students to divide in half and go around. Herbie had to double back to him.

"Are you serious?" Worser asked.

Herbie nodded. "Yep." He glanced up at a clock on the wall. "Aw, man. Nanna's probably already here. Last week I was late leaving the building and we got in trouble for blocking the pickup lane. See you tomorrow!" He turned and jogged down the hallway, his figure becoming a curly-haired silhouette as he approached the sun-drenched glass doors.

Worser continued toward the library. Sure enough, the interior windows revealed it to be dark and empty. A note printed in large, Arial Black font had been taped to the door:

**ATTENTION STUDENTS:
THE LIBRARY WILL BE LOCKED AFTER SCHOOL UNTIL FURTHER NOTICE.
IF YOU NEED TO RETURN MATERIALS, PLEASE USE THE BOOK DROP ON THE WALL TO THE RIGHT.**

A boy stood reading the sign—a boy for whom *boy* would not quite be the correct term. He was obviously an eighth grader, although he looked even older, with his broad shoulders and smatterings of pencil-mark-like whiskers on his cheeks and chin. He was also over a foot taller, so Worser found himself staring straight at the individual's Adam's apple—both spellbound and unsettled by the knotty protrusion and the way it jutted outward, as if it were a dowel connecting the head to the neck. It made Worser swallow reflexively.

He knew this man-boy in that vague way of having shared the same educational institution with him for a year. He'd noticed him before, possibly had a class with him, or maybe he'd been tormented by him. If Worser wasn't feeling so intimidated, he could probably recall the male creature's name. He knew it was some single-syllable moniker with lots of saliva-producing consonants. Kurt? Mac? Brock?

"Man. This sucks," the man-boy said, gazing at the sign on the door.

Nick? Rick?

"Total tyrannage," the teen titan continued, shaking his shaggy head.

Worser couldn't help himself. "Tyrannage?"

"Yeah, man. Like tyranny. They're keeping us down." He began loping away.

That's when the name came to Worser. "Turk."

Turk turned. "Yeah?"

"Um…" Worser hadn't meant to say it aloud. He quickly scanned his memories but couldn't come up with an instance of past harassment by this person—although he knew that most males of this age and size were capable of it. "Just…sorry. About…the tyrannage."

Turk smiled. "Fist bump," he said, and punched the air between them.

FOUR

Accommodations

Worser had hoped to kill some time at the school library before he headed home. He knew the therapists had emphasized how important it was to stick to a routine, to help facilitate his mother's memory, but sometimes it was hard to stay on a schedule, especially if it meant going somewhere you weren't always happy to be.

Aunt Iris had purchased an enormous monthly calendar with tear-off sheets and hung it in the dining room. In each day square, she would write scheduled activities in large print and pair them with cartoon figures of each person involved. Next to the three regular therapy appointments on Mondays, Wednesdays, and Fridays from 10:00 a.m. to 1:00 p.m., she drew a stick figure with straight hair for his mom and one with curly hair for herself.

On school days, next to the times Worser typically left home and returned, she always drew a baseball-cap-wearing boy (which he found both ludicrous and misleading, since he'd never in his life worn a baseball cap). And at the end of each day, Aunt Iris would routinely, and somewhat ceremoniously,

X out the square with a maroon marker to help his mother grasp the passage of time. Worser hated the sight. All those red slash marks—all those bloodshot reminders of time spent in this new upside-down reality.

That morning he'd noticed Aunt Iris had written in today's square, "Take Potato clothes shopping?" She had been on him for some time about the worn condition of his clothing and insisted it was tradition to buy new back-to-school outfits—a tradition Worser felt was nothing but manipulative commercialism. Why should he care if his pants and shirts were faded or had loose threads? All that mattered was that he was adequately covered. And he was.

He wanted to grab a snack and go relax in his room—but the note made him wary. No doubt the second he arrived he'd be pressured into some traumatic shopping trip, with Aunt Iris's hooting laugh drawing attention to them and strangers shooting pitying looks at his mother.

It infuriated him that his aunt kept trying to parent him. Of course, these efforts weren't new, since she'd often brought or mailed him clothes over the years (including the Calvin and Hobbes shirt that Herbie so admired last year), but at least her gifts had spared him the indignity of having to shop with her.

As Worser stepped onto the porch past the thicket of half-dead spider plants, he could hear...music? And...laughter? Careful to avoid the loose, creaky planks, he made his way to the window.

Music was blaring from some unseen spot, no doubt one of his aunt's gadgets. An irritating mesh of noise—all *blang* and *crash* and *bombitty*. He couldn't even make out the words the singer was screeching. Of course, if he could understand them, he'd almost certainly find them maudlin and clunky, rhyming *kiss* with *missed* or *heavenly* with *seven seas*.

Aunt Iris was holding onto his mother's hands, making her arms sway back and forth, giggling like a child one-sixth her actual age. Together they shuffled their feet, turning in a slow circle. Eventually, his mother's face came into view. Mouth in a wide-open smile—higher on the left side. Head bobbing, not because of the rhythm of the song, but because of her lack of muscle control.

He wasn't sure what he was seeing at first, but then it came to him: dancing. Aunt Iris was making his mother dance!

Worser felt embarrassed for her. Dr. Constance Orser, dancing and grinning like a buffoon? He was ashamed to have even glimpsed it. A wave of fury took him over, and he visualized himself racing into the house, breaking the offending gadget, and yelling at his aunt for subjecting his mom to this degradation. Instead, he turned and ran away.

If he'd had his wits about him, he would have headed to his secret spot in the tree. But, alas, that handy part of his mind that managed planning and reason wasn't operating. All control had been handed to a smaller, less sophisticated part of his brain that simply urged him to *go*—to put as much distance between himself and the house as possible.

While such an instinct to flee might impel other creatures for miles, Worser gave out after a couple of blocks. He was tired. He was sweating. His backpack was heavy. He needed a snack. The urgency that powered him was waning, but he still didn't want to turn around and trudge back to his house.

He slowly spun in a circle, scanning his surroundings, and recognized the obnoxious orange neon U-BAG'M sign in the shopping center not far from his house. Generally, he and his mother avoided places that butchered spelling, grammar, or punctuation (and this establishment achieved the trifecta), but he was feeling desperate. Ten minutes later, Worser was stepping out of the U-Bag'M with a large Gulpee drink—flavor unknown. The crushed ice was covered in an electric-blue liquid that at times tasted like coconut and other times tasted like bubble gum. It was refreshing nonetheless and went nicely with his "grande"-sized cheese stick.

Soon, he was done eating and all that was left of his drink was a small mound of aquamarine-colored slush. Noisily slurping through the straw, he pivoted once again in a slow circle. He knew he should go home, and yet he couldn't. Literally. The mere recollection of his mother dancing like an unsteady, wide-eyed toddler locked his limbs and prevented him from even facing in that direction for longer than an instant.

It was Aunt Iris's fault. Talk about "tyrannage"! Over the past weeks he'd come to understand why he and his mother used to see her just on holidays and birthdays—even though she only lived fifty miles away in Denton. Once, when he'd asked his mother about their relationship, she'd replied with a sigh, "Iris is better in small, infrequent doses."

Now Aunt Iris was with his mother all day, every day. To make matters worse, she appeared to be trying to remake his mother into a second version of herself under the guise of helping her heal. She, the younger sister, was suddenly the one in charge and was claiming the right to reorder their house and their lives. And Worser felt out of place everywhere—even on his own premises.

But if he couldn't face home, where could he go?

And just like that, the instant the question entered his mind, Worser got a sign from above—in the form of an actual sign hanging over his head. He was standing at the base of a tall metal pole, the top of which listed the stores in the shopping center, and his eyes locked on to one beloved word: BOOK. Somewhere nearby was a place called Re-Visions Used Books. Tossing his cup and wrapper into a metal trash bin, he located the storefront and made a beeline across the parking lot toward it.

Worser stepped into the store, his arrival announced by a strip of bells hanging on the opposite side of the door. Once inside, he paused to take in the surroundings, a strange calm seeping over him.

The store was laid out in the shape of a capital *L*. For *Literature*. Or *Learning*. Or *Lair*. The bottom part of the *L*, where he now stood, held racks of children's books, paperbacks, and magazines facing the windows. On his right was a sales counter with a man sitting atop a high stool behind the register. Behind that was a dim hallway with an EMPLOYEES ONLY sign over the doorway. But it was the other part of the *L* that made up most of the store and captivated Worser. He could see bookcases lined against the wall on the left and more that stretched out in rows facing him—each filled with books of every color and thickness. Countless numbers of words in countless combinations. All of them beckoning to him.

He wondered if this was how explorers felt when they stumbled upon unfamiliar lands.

"Excuse me, sir," he said to the man behind the counter, "has this place been here long?"

"What are you? A reporter?"

"I've just never heard about it."

"What every business owner wants to hear."

Worser wandered up and down the aisles with his hand out, enjoying the feel of his fingertips gliding over the little speed bumps of the book spines. As he rounded the third and final row of bookcases, he came across a rectangular oak table, neatly hidden in the back of the store. His mouth curved into a small smile.

He returned to the man behind the counter. "Sir? Could I sit at the table in the back and work on a project?"

"Kid, this isn't a library. If you're going to read a book, you have to buy the book."

"Actually, I'm going to be writing. Might I sit there for that?"

"That table is for paying customers only."

Worser cast his gaze about until he spotted a worthy item. "I'll buy this pocket dictionary."

The man let out a long sigh. "Fine. But don't be a nuisance, all right? I like things quiet."

"There won't be any problems."

Again, Worser realized he was smiling. He found the place comforting. The bookcases overflowing with stock, some books stuck on top of others, oversized or odd-shaped tomes leaning every which way on the bottom shelves. The way dust toned down the colors and swirled in the sunlight angling in from the front window. The musty, woody smell. He even delighted in the gruff disposition of the store owner. It reminded him of home—the way home used to be before Aunt Iris showed up with her bright clothing, incense, and proclivity toward cleaning.

Worser studied the store owner as he rang up the purchase. The man was compact and slightly hunched. He was bald on top, but his bushy brows and the thick hair on the sides of his head stuck out in all directions—especially the coarser gray hairs. That plus the dark blazer he wore over his faded blue button-down made Worser think of a crested penguin.

"Thank you, sir," he said as the man handed him his new-used pocket dictionary.

"Meh."

Worser trotted back to the table, sat down, and started to pull items from his backpack. Newspapers were strewn all over, some folded, some untouched.

"Sir?" he called out. "Is it all right if I move these papers so I can spread out my materials on the table? I won't take up the whole surface."

The man uttered a syllable that sounded like *gah*. "Quit calling me *sir* like I'm some Knight of the Round Table. It's Mr. Murray. In fact, just quit calling out, period. You promised to be quiet, and I expected that to take hold immediately. I'll let you know if you do anything wrong. Sheesh."

Worser stacked the newspapers in a corner of the table and finished unloading his backpack. Figuring he'd get his assignment out of the way before starting on his Masterwork, he pulled out his geography homework. Just as he suspected, he immediately noticed the sad man in profile when he looked at Montana's western border—and figured he probably would from now on.

He had just started to fill in the states on the unmarked map when inspiration struck. He grabbed his Masterwork binder and turned to a blank sheet. At the top of the page, he wrote out a new title: Words Comprised of State Abbreviations. Below that, he added the abbreviations in alphabetical order, followed by a brief list of ground rules.

He quickly noticed that some abbreviations were words unto themselves, like HI, ID, IN, OH, OK, the musical term MI, and PA. Fingertips sparking, he began to combine the abbreviations into larger words. As he worked, the physical world receded, replaced by words, paper, patterns, and the excited whir of his nervous system.

After a ninety-minute stretch, he'd compiled a fairly long list:

AL AK AZ AR CA CO CT DE FL GA HI ID IL IN IA KS KY LA ME MD MA MI MN MS MO MT NE NV NH NJ NM NY NC ND OH OK OR PA RI SC SD TN TX UT VT VA WA WV WI WY

Rules:
1. State abbreviations must be used whole; they cannot be divided.
2. State abbreviations must remain in their correct order. No reversing CA to AC, etc.
3. No other letters may be added to the words—they must *only* be made up of the abbreviations.
4. It is permissible to repeat a state abbreviation in a word, as in DECODE.
5. No proper nouns, abbreviations, or new slang.

AL	CT	LA
alarms	DE	laid
alms	deal	lain
almond	dear	lame
alpaca	decade	land
AK	decode	lane
akin	demand	late
AZ	deny	lava
AR	deride	ME
aria	FL	meal
arid	flak	memorial
arms	floral	mend
arcade	florid	MD
arcane	GA	MA
CA	gain	maid
came	gala	main
candid	game	mane
candor	HI	many
cane	hind	MI
CO	ID	mica
coal	IL	mime
code	IN	mind
coil	inky	MN
coin	income	MS
cola	inlaid	MO
coma	inland	moor
come	invade	moms
condor	IA	MT
cone	KS	NE
cook	KY	near

<u>NV</u>	pail	<u>VT</u>
<u>NH</u>	pain	<u>VA</u>
<u>NJ</u>	pane	vain
<u>NM</u>	<u>RI</u>	vandal
<u>NY</u>	ride	<u>WA</u>
<u>NC</u>	rims	wade
<u>ND</u>	rind	wand
<u>OH</u>	rite	wane
<u>OK</u>	<u>SC</u>	wail
<u>OR</u>	scar	wend
oral	<u>SD</u>	wind
ordeal	<u>TN</u>	<u>WV</u>
<u>PA</u>	<u>TX</u>	<u>WI</u>
pact	<u>UT</u>	wide
		<u>WY</u>

It had been weeks since he'd been this productive. He felt breathless, almost light-headed, and his lips were wet from his habit of distractedly pushing his tongue against the corners of his mouth.

Worser took a moment to think of a word that might describe his emotional state. *Satisfied?* Not strong enough. *Elated?* Not quite right either.

Contented. That was it. *Con* for *concentration, contemplation,* and the *control* he felt over his situation. *Ed,* a suggestion of past tense and an expression of hope that the tension he'd been experiencing could be left in the past. And right in the middle of the word, *tent,* a shelter—protection from conditions and creatures that might thwart him. He was so grateful for this austere and secluded workspace, the thought of leaving pained him.

Worser packed up his belongings and trotted to the

counter. "Mr. Murray? Could I work out an arrangement with you? I'd like to rent this worktable a couple of weekdays after school—on Mondays, Wednesdays, and occasional other days with prior notice. What hourly rate would be appropriate in your view?"

Mr. Murray fixed him with the same expression from before. Not so much angry as cramped.

"You're kind of a weirdo, aren't you?"

Worser wasn't sure how to respond. It seemed more like an observation than a question.

"But you work quietly. I like that." The man rubbed the fuzzy patch of gray whiskers that stood out on his chin like dandelion spores. He seemed in favor of the idea—judging by the minor smoothing of his brow—so Worser was surprised when he finally said, "Nah. That sounds like the sort of deal that could get me in trouble. I got enough problems, kid."

"We could write up a contract."

"Ah, who wants to mess with something like that? What a nuisance."

"Then how about..." Worser's gaze bounced around, looking for an answer. "How about I purchase at least ten dollars' worth of books for every hour I'm here? And since I likely won't need them or have room in my backpack, I'll immediately donate them back to the store. That way you'll make sales but not lose stock."

Mr. Murray raised his bristled chin and frowned off into the distance. His lips moved ever so slightly, as if counting to himself. Worser, meanwhile, was practically hopping in place. He *had to* make this work.

Finally, Mr. Murray leaned forward and stared Worser right in the eyes. "And you'll be quiet?"

"I will."

"Then I guess we have ourselves a deal."

Worser nodded and headed out the door. Once again, a sense of peace came over him, magnified by the knowledge that this would not be a one-time event. And it would only cost him a minor rental fee each time.

Thank goodness he had some money: funds kept in an interest-bearing account at the local bank. His parents had set it up for him when he was born and had a percentage of their pay automatically deposited each month; then, ever since his father died, some Social Security money had been put in every month. When he was old enough, his mother had given him a prepaid debit card, and because he only used it for supplies and infrequent binges on junk food from the corner gas station, his balance had grown considerably.

In fact, the last time he'd checked—before the purchase of his after-school snacks and the dictionary—Worser's account held $57,343.72.

As soon as he walked through the front door, Aunt Iris pounced on him.

"Where have you been? We've been frantic with worry!"

"I was shopping." He walked past her into the kitchen.

Aunt Iris followed. "Shopping? For what?"

"A book."

"A book?"

Worser was becoming increasingly annoyed at his aunt's insistence on repeating his responses in a high-pitched, grating voice. "Yes."

"A book," she said again. "For this whole time? What kind of a book?"

"It doesn't matter."

Aunt Iris turned away from him, both hands raised, her head shaking back and forth making her earrings jingle. "Your mother is asleep, probably because she was worn out from being so distressed. We were worried you'd been hurt on your walk home from school! I was about to call the hospitals."

"You're being dramatic."

"How can you say that? You should have been here two hours ago. Why didn't you call?"

Worser could only blink at her. It hadn't occurred to him to call. His mother had never questioned him when he stayed late at the library after school or disappeared to his tree house. And if his mother didn't worry about such things, why should his aunt?

"You didn't check the calendar, did you?" Aunt Iris's voice was back to her regular tone of disappointment. "Oh, Potato. You've got to get into the habit of checking it every morning."

Worser didn't want to tell her that he had, in fact, checked the calendar and saw her plan to purchase him new clothes, but it had not motivated him to race home.

"Your mother's physical therapy appointment was canceled—just for today while they finished up some repairs. So instead, she and I did a little movement therapy after her nap. Oh, we had lots of fun." Aunt Iris's smile slowly vanished as she heaved one of her lengthy and, in Worser's opinion, highly theatrical sighs. "We'd been hoping to all go to the department store as soon as you got home, but then you never showed up."

Worser also didn't want to tell her that he actually had made it home on time, but the sight of Aunt Iris and his mother dancing had driven him away.

"We waited and waited and worried and worried," she went on. "This is why you should have a cell phone."

"Never." Worser crossed his arms over his chest and straightened up as high as his fifty-four-and-a-half-inch frame could go. "They're responsible for the deterioration of language. Besides, they're radioactive. Mom agrees with me on this."

"I know she does."

"Also, I've told you several times that I don't need new clothes. And I don't appreciate your keeping tabs on my whereabouts. Mom never did as long as I was home for dinner. It isn't any of your concern as far as I can see."

"Actually...," Aunt Iris began, then let the word trail off. "Potato, I promise, this isn't me being nosy. I would like to know where you will be in case anything happens with your mother that you should know about."

"Like what?" A dull panic rose up inside him.

"Nothing in particular. But if your mother needs you, I'd like to be able to find you."

Worser realized, reluctantly, that his aunt had a point.

He exhaled in defeat. "Fine," he said. "Then you should know that if I'm not here on Mondays and Wednesdays, I will likely be at Re-Visions Used Books at the shopping center. The library is now closed after school, so I made an arrangement with the proprietor. He's letting me write and read at a table there on Monday and Wednesday afternoons. That environment is far more conducive to studying than this house, with all the constant interruptions by you and your belligerent animals. But no cell phone."

He braced himself for an argument. He was prepared to

yell if he had to—to stomp and curse and toss things onto the floor.

His comings and goings were none of her business. She was not his mother.

"Very well, then," Aunt Iris said breezily. "Please add it to the calendar." And she whirled out of view.

FIVE

Occupation

Two days later Worser was back in the principal's office, in the same stiff-backed chair.

Across from him, Principal Ludlum let out a sigh and said, "Excrement. On a paper. It is yours, correct?"

"The paper or the excrement?"

"This is not the time to be funny."

"I was merely being precise. It is my paper. It is a cat's excrement."

"Why on earth did you turn in your assignment for English covered in...feces?"

"It was due today."

"Surely you don't expect Ms. Fife to accept a paper in such a condition."

"I felt I had no choice. When I discovered it this morning, there was no time to remedy the situation or I would have been tardy—which is also frowned upon." He tilted his head, filled with a new thought. "Are you going to call my aunt?"

Another sigh. "We might not have to. She has been calling us fairly regularly."

"She has?" Worser frowned. "Why?"

"She's concerned about you." Mr. Ludlum paused, but Worser just held his stare. "Of course, we're *all* concerned," the principal went on, straightening a stack of files on his desk. "We're hoping to see you more engaged in life. It's a pity you aren't active in clubs or sports. I myself enjoyed swimming when I was your age."

Worser shifted his gaze, concentrating on the carpeting, the whorls of wood grain in the desktop—anything that would block out thoughts of Mr. Ludlum swimming.

With an educator parent, Worser had never been one of those youngsters who assumed his teachers slept at school. And yet there could be no other backdrop for Mr. Ludlum. If he were a paper doll, the only choice would be to dress him in an ill-fitting suit and set him behind a too-big desk. Any other option—on a surfboard, holding a banjo, eating a sub sandwich, driving a race car—would be too absurd to bear.

Freed from Worser's scrutiny, Mr. Ludlum seemed inspired to keep talking. "It's important that every child find their place here at school—something that makes them feel motivated, part of something bigger than themselves. There are many groups and activities available to you. If you were to join a club, perhaps you'd feel better. Then there'd be no need for our little visits like this one and the one last week."

Worser once again fixed his eyes upon the principal and raised his left eyebrow. Mr. Ludlum swallowed.

"I used to have a place here at school," Worser said. "I had the library. That was where I felt I belonged. I could read and write and feel inspired to work on important projects. And my 'little visits' began when you called me in here last week *because* I went there instead of the pep rally. Now the library has been deemed off-limits after school."

"Yes, well, I'm sorry. But, you see, my hands are tied." Mr. Ludlum shrugged and lifted his open, untied hands. "The librarian, Ms. Petrie, now splits time with another campus and will only be here in the mornings. There's simply no one qualified who's available to provide supervision after school. I understand what you're saying, but I'm afraid I'm at the mercy of budget cuts and other decisions by the powers that be."

"And *I* understand what *you're* saying," Worser said, "but I'm afraid I'm at the mercy of two partly feral cats who don't like me and can't find the litter box."

At Re-Visions after school, he spent two hours creating words out of the chemical symbols—inspired by his work with the state abbreviations. It was exhilarating to disappear into the logic of letter combinations while sitting in the stillness and quiet of the bookstore. When Worser had said hello, Mr. Murray had grunted in reply and didn't speak to him after that.

By the end of his stay, Worser had completely forgotten about movements of time and his sullied reputation with his English teacher. He had only gotten through words beginning with elements one through five—hydrogen (H) through carbon (C)—and knew there were still dozens more he could find. Worser picked out two crossword-puzzle books, which Mr. Murray rang up silently; then he donated them back to the store. As he walked home, he continued combining letters in his head. He was in such a state of concentration when he entered the house that Aunt Iris's voice barely registered.

"Oh, there you are. I hope you got a lot done at the store," she said as she followed Worser into the kitchen—her words only faintly reaching him, as if she were calling from a distant hilltop. "We had an exciting day. Your mother is lying down resting while I make dinner."

Her prattle was like the treble melody to the refrigerator's low steady hum and the rhythmic swishing of the dishwasher. Worser could hear it, but it remained in the background, not truly penetrating his mind.

As he grabbed a bag of pretzels and headed toward the living room, he heard her call out, "Wait! Dinner will be ready soon. And please don't eat in there. My p-ohms are there, and some of them are still wet."

The last sentence jolted him out of his daze. "Poems?" he asked, pausing before rounding the corner.

"Yes," Aunt Iris said. "They arrived today. I just put a fresh coat of paint on two of them."

Worser looked stricken. "When did you start writing poetry? And what kinds of poems get painted and take up a room?"

"No. Not poetry," Aunt Iris said. "You saw them at my apartment. Remember? They're p-ohms. That is, each one is a p-ohm: *p*, hyphen, *o*, *h*, *m*. My usable art pieces. I had them sent from home."

"What on earth is 'usable art'? And what does a measurement of electrical resistance have to do with it?"

Aunt Iris laughed. "No. Not that kind of *ohm*. The *p* is for *private*, and *ohm* is the mantra people repeat in meditation. Sometimes it's spelled *o, m*. Or *a, u, m*."

"I still don't understand."

"Come see."

He set his bag on the counter and followed her.

"Voilà!" Aunt Iris cried. She let out a childlike laugh and

gestured theatrically into their living room—which now resembled the hull of a cargo ship.

Ah yes. He remembered these atrocities. All around the room sat wooden packing crates, approximately three and a half feet high, equally wide, and five feet long. Most were painted in vibrant jewel tones—violet, deep purple, indigo blue, or emerald green—then further decorated with stars, curlicues, scroll patterns, or medallion-like designs that, Aunt Iris had once explained, were called *mandalas*. She left one end of the crate open as an entrance and covered it with strips of gauzy fabric or beaded curtains. Worser had sometimes seen her working on them—often in the middle of the night—during those weeks in the summer when he stayed with her. She was a self-professed night owl, and he, at the time, couldn't sleep after long days spent worried and frustrated.

"We have to keep a close eye out for the cats," she said, peering into one of the crates. "Ging thinks Forgiveness belongs to her. I always find her napping in there. It will really hurt my chances of selling it to someone who might have allergies."

"Forgiveness?"

"Yes. That one there." She pointed to a box painted the color of the chamomile tea she constantly drank that was highlighted with silvery heart shapes. A dark burgundy drape shuttered the interior from view.

"They have names?"

"Oh yes. There's Truth over there and Joy just there."

"I don't understand. What are they *for*?"

Aunt Iris seemed to grow a half inch. "Oh! It's wonderful. Here, try one." She held open the green velvet fabric covering the nearest work in progress and urged Worser to go inside.

"Enter and face the opposite side," she instructed. "Then kneel or sit with your legs crossed."

"And do what?"

"Just be."

"That makes no sense. I'm always *being*. If I were to stop being, I would be dead. You're saying you want me to go in there and... not die?"

"I want you to sit and think. Or meditate."

Despite himself, Worser found that he wanted to understand. He crawled inside the crate and discovered that the "floor" was decently cushioned. It took a moment to fold himself up, but eventually he managed a position that seemed bearable—if not exactly comfortable. "Now what?" he asked.

"Concentrate on the mantra in front of you."

"Mantra?"

"The message. The hymn."

He stared straight ahead. Painted in fancy script on the "wall" before him was the word *Release*. "It just looks as if that side of the box is an emergency exit."

Aunt Iris knelt beside the crate and whispered encouragements through the curtain. "You can do this. Meditate on the concept of letting go. How we often hold onto things we shouldn't, or hold onto things too tightly, when it's far better to surrender our grasp."

Her instructions only heightened Worser's unease. "That's irresponsible. Holding on prevents falling. It stops things from slipping out of our hands and breaking."

"True. But you can't hold onto everything. Some things you have to let go. Just like we can't only take in a breath. We have to eventually let it out."

"Speaking of letting something out..." Worser had to

grab hold of his legs and tug a few times. Soon he unfurled and backed out of the crate.

"Well? What do you think?" his aunt asked once he'd gotten to his feet.

He shook his head. "It makes no sense to read one word over and over."

"Oh, but it's not reading. It's visualizing. Plus, there's the silence. After all, silence is wise, and the spaces between words are just as important as the words. Ahhh." Aunt Iris opened her arms. "I'm so glad they finally arrived. Now I can finish my pieces and sell them from here. Isn't that wonderful?"

"No. They're ludicrous, and they take up too much room."

Aunt Iris's arms plopped back down to her sides. "Why do you have to be unkind?"

"I'm concerned that you're wasting your time and filling my home with junk."

Aunt Iris gaped at him. Worser noticed the ridiculous gold stud in her nose, above her right nostril, and the thin, unused paintbrush tucked inexplicably behind her left ear. He was just wondering if she was using this tense break in the conversation to demonstrate the wisdom of silence when she took a deep, necklace-rattling breath.

"Don't tell me," she began, "that you are suddenly worried about cleanliness. When I arrived, this house was filled with grime and old papers. I found a *New York Times* from 2004. Seer found a petrified mouse under a stack of journals from the 1990s! So forgive me if I don't believe you're truly worried about the fact that my artwork is making the space a little more confined!" As she spoke, Aunt Iris's voice had taken on the same jarring drone of a paper shredder—and evoked in Worser the same faint, ill-defined fear.

Worser knew he couldn't argue her point. He and his mother had never been big on cleaning and organizing. He hadn't thought much about it until Aunt Iris started staying there in late July after his mother was released from the rehab facility. She would ask things like "Which cabinet holds the spices?" or "Where do you keep the scissors?" It had never occurred to him—and, perhaps, his mother—to assign specific places for everything or designate a drawer or cupboard for certain types of items. It took a week to find the vacuum cleaner. And when they did (in his mother's closet under a pile of clothes and coats), his aunt called it a museum piece—which might have seemed like a compliment coming from a self-professed artist, but he could tell it wasn't.

Aunt Iris placed her fingertips on his right shoulder. "I'm sorry," she said, her voice back to normal volume. "I haven't been sleeping well—not that that's any excuse. I should be practicing better self-care."

Self-care. The term was part of the vocabulary he'd learned from his aunt over the years, along with *mindfulness, centering, karma,* and *kefir*—words that he'd never found a use for.

"Why don't you go check in on your mom? I think I'm going to spend a few more moments here."

Worser watched as she crawled into a different crate, the one she'd referred to as Forgiveness, and disappeared behind the curtain.

"Oh, by the way." Her head partly reappeared. "Your mom's friend called and invited us to dinner this Friday night."

"Friend?" Worser was suspicious. His mother had relationships with people the way he did—which is to say, very few and on a limited basis.

"That nice man who visited in the hospital? The one she teaches with."

"Professor Khoury?"

"Yes, that's the one. I told him your mother would likely be too tired from her therapy sessions and that I'd need to be available to her, so he suggested you come alone. I told him you'd like that. I hope that's all right."

"I, um,... Yes, that's all right."

She nodded, and the curtain flap closed again.

Dinner at the Khoury house. Donya Khoury's house. Friday. Worser was simultaneously astonished and panic-stricken—and grateful to his aunt for agreeing to it.

"Aunt Iris?"

She peered back out, looking concerned. "Yes?"

"P-ohms. I do like the play on words. Very clever."

Her features softened. "Thank you," she said, and vanished into Forgiveness.

SIX

Courtesy

This would not be Worser's first visit to the Khoury home. The first dinner had taken place back when he was four, not long after his dad had died in his sleep and only a month after the office encounter when young Donya had commented on his intelligence. He could still recall how he'd felt that evening when he and his mother arrived, how excited he'd been to see Donya again. Earlier that day his mother had taken him to the doctor, where he'd learned a smart-sounding new word, and he had been eager to share it with everyone. Thus, the first full sentence little Worser had ever said directly to Donya was "I have an infection!"

He wanted desperately to believe he'd gotten better at casual conversation, but he feared he hadn't. Even so, the Khourys kept inviting them over, and his mother accepted once or twice a year.

Aunt Iris had advised him to "dress nice," but when he came downstairs in maroon corduroys and a faded orange polo that was tight across his chest, she blinked and said, "Don't you have anything else?"

Worser suppressed his impulse to argue. Exasperating as

it was to have Aunt Iris fuss about him, he knew she was his only hope at looking decent for Donya.

"Where are the button-down shirts I gave you last year for Christmas?" she asked.

"Dirty."

"What do you mean? I never saw them in your hamper."

"There's another place. In the laundry room."

He led her out to the garage-utility room and showed her the cardboard box their new (now five-year-old) dishwasher had arrived in, where he and his mother would deposit dirty clothes when they began to overtake their respective rooms.

"Lord have mercy!" Aunt Iris exclaimed after upending the box and discovering that the pile had retained its cube-like shape. "How long have these been sitting here, unwashed?"

Worser shrugged. He honestly had no idea.

"Never mind. We'll find something else."

Fifteen minutes later they were pulling up in front of the Khourys' house. Worser was wearing jeans and a slightly faded, somewhat-too-big dusty blue Oxford that had belonged to his dad.

Aunt Iris had asked him to sit in the back seat next to his mom, and he'd done so without complaint. During the ride, he'd noticed his mother seemed smaller than she'd been before the stroke. Perhaps it was because she was stooped and tired from the day's therapy sessions even though she'd had her nap. Collette, the health-care worker who'd provided daily in-home care after his mother had first been released from the nursing home, once explained that intense fatigue was one of the greatest factors among stroke patients. "Naps for months," she'd said.

Worser reached for the door handle.

"Be sure to ask if you can help set the table," Aunt Iris said. His expression must have revealed his confusion, for she elaborated. "It's polite for guests to offer to help in some small way, to thank their hosts for all the effort made on their behalf. Dr. Khoury even agreed to drop you off after dinner, since Constance will likely be in bed by then."

"Beh," said his mother.

"Yes, bed. Very good, Constance!" Aunt Iris clapped.

Worser wanted to admonish her for treating his mother like an infant, but he bit his tongue. Despite his annoyance, he was thankful that his aunt had agreed to his attending dinner at Donya's, thankful that she'd found him appropriate attire, and thankful for the ride over.

"Have a good time, Potato!"

As soon as he opened the car door, Aunt Iris called out, "Wait! I almost forgot!" She lifted a white cardboard box from the passenger seat and handed it to him. "Here's dessert. It's customary to bring something for your hosts."

He glanced at his mom to see if she registered any lunacy in the situation—bringing food to people who offered to feed you. But she continued to sit quietly, head tilting ever so slightly.

"Be good, okay?" Aunt Iris said with a wave. "And have fun! We'll see you in a few hours."

Worser climbed from the car, carrying the box, his mind spinning as he tried to remember all the rules of conduct his aunt had explained. It was surprisingly difficult to walk, hold a dessert, and think at the same time.

Luckily, he made it safely to the front stoop. Once there, an appalling sight made him forget everything: the doormat. The roughly woven rectangle had once read WELCOME HOME, but after years of use and exposure to weather, a few letters had faded so that it now read ME HOME. He'd noticed it on his last visit, a year earlier, and was bothered by the ungrammatical (though accidental) sentence. Its continued existence offended him.

Dr. Khoury answered the door. He had the same thick wavy hair and wide horizontal smile as Donya. "Hello," he said.

"You need a new doormat," Worser said.

"Oh?" Dr. Khoury glanced down at the mat and laughed nervously. "Well, yes. Yes, I suppose we do."

Worser handed him the white box.

"Is this for us?" Dr. Khoury asked. "What is it?"

"It's dessert, but I don't know what it is," Worser replied truthfully. "I think it's to say thank you. For feeling sorry for me."

Dr. Khoury's smile fell away. At the same moment, Mrs. Khoury appeared beside him in the doorframe.

"William! So good to see you. Come in, come in." She turned sideways and waved her hand in small circles.

Each time he walked through the Khourys' front door, Worser was surprised by the differences between their house and his own. Theirs wasn't overrun with clutter the way his was. Nor did it have the tabletop fountains, potted succulents, and crocheted knickknacks of his aunt's apartment—the only other residence where he'd spent a significant amount of time. Instead, the Khourys' place had an air of meaning and self-consciousness. Everything in it seemed imbued with a history, carefully chosen, and deliberately arranged. The antique clock that let out somber chimes on the hour. The burgundy rug with the intricate, colorful pattern laid over the knotted beige carpeting in the living room. The walls that displayed framed family photos, diplomas, and rudimentary paintings he suspected were done by Donya and her younger brother, Seth. At his own house, the only thing on the wall was a faded sign taped up in the bathroom that read WIGGLE HANDLE AFTER FLUSHING.

"I'm so glad you could join us this evening." Mrs. Khoury's smile went up rather than across, lifting her cheeks and creating beautiful creases around her eyes, like decorative fringe. Donya had her eyes, only brown instead of blue and minus the embellishing lines.

"William brought key-lime pie," Dr. Khoury exclaimed, having opened the dessert box.

"How nice!" Mrs. Khoury said, taking the box. "I'll just go pop it in the fridge for later." She trotted through a nearby doorway.

Dr. Khoury kept smiling and nodding—a nervous gesture Donya referred to as "bobblehead Dad." Worser had asked her about it on one of his previous visits. "He does that with everyone," she'd told him.

"Make yourself at home," Dr. Khoury said. "Our casa is your casa." As he waved Worser into the living room, his gestures seemed exaggerated, his speech punctuated by loud, needless laughter.

"Thanks."

"So, how's your mother?" he asked. "I hope she's improving."

"My aunt says she is."

"Ah, good. It's good your aunt is there. Good woman. Yes. We all miss your mom back at the college. Yes." Nod. Nod. Nod.

Mrs. Khoury reappeared and ushered them both through the living room toward the kitchen, saying, "We aren't ready just yet. Come in and join us as we finish up." Worser and Dr. Khoury fell into step behind her, Worser glancing around for Donya.

"William is here," Mrs. Khoury announced as they walked into the kitchen. Donya stood hunched over a cutting board. "Donya is our salad chef."

"Just because I have major knife skills," Donya muttered. "I do like hacking at things."

"Honey, take your hoodie off. It looks like you're about to leave."

"Mom, no. I'm keeping it on."

Mrs. Khoury opened her mouth as if to protest, then appeared to change her mind and went back to transferring pieces of chicken onto a serving dish. Meanwhile Donya continued chopping mushrooms and Dr. Khoury stirred something in a pot on the stove.

Worser stood there, watching them, unsure of what to do. Then he remembered his aunt's suggestion. "Might I help set the table?"

Mrs. Khoury grinned at him. "That would be nice. Thank you."

"I already did the plates and glasses," Dr. Khoury said. "But could you lay out the silverware?"

"I'm fairly confident I could do that," Worser replied.

Their laughter surprised him, as he hadn't been making a joke.

Mrs. Khoury handed him a wire caddy full of flatware, and Worser pushed through the swinging door to the formal dining room.

A dark wood table stood before him covered in a lacy tablecloth. On it lay five cream-colored placemats, each topped with a gold-rimmed white plate, a glass tumbler full of ice, and a deep gold cloth napkin rolled up like a tiny newspaper. Worser pulled out a fork and marveled at how shiny it was—and how every utensil in the caddy matched, each with tiny roses stamped into the handle.

Bourgeois, a voice said in his head. His mother's voice. His brain had spun up a memory from one of their dinner visits a few years earlier. She'd used the word on the drive home when he asked about the decorative tissue-box covers and the shaggy covering on the toilet lid. *Boxes for boxes! Covers for covers!* They'd chuckled the rest of the way home.

A sound yanked Worser back to the present.

"Pssst!"

Donya was in the room with him, setting the salad on the table.

"Forks have to go on the left, knives and spoons on the right," she whispered.

"Why?" Worser asked.

"Because otherwise the world would die," she said, rolling her eyes.

Worser felt the corners of his mouth tugging upward. He wondered if she ever used the word *bourgeois*.

Just as he placed the last knife at the last place setting, Dr. and Mrs. Khoury came into the room, carrying platters of food. "All right," Mrs. Khoury said. "No need to wait for Seth. There's no telling when he'll be back from his soccer game. Let's go ahead and start." This prompted a flurry of new activity. Chicken, vegetables, salad dressing, and a basket of rolls were set in the center of the table. Someone took the utensil caddy from his hands. Donya left and returned with a pitcher of iced tea. Chairs were noisily pulled away from the table. Worser stepped out of the way and watched, impressed by the choreography.

As the four of them took their seats, the front door burst open and Seth barreled in wearing his soccer uniform. "Bye, Nicholas!" he shouted behind him before shutting the door and racing up the stairs.

Mrs. Khoury strode to the bottom of the stairs and called, "Seth? Wash up and come down to dinner. We have company."

Five minutes later, Seth reappeared in khaki shorts, a white T-shirt, and earbuds. "*Ehh, ehh, ehh!*" Dr. Khoury said, imitating some sort of warning buzzer. He pulled out one of the earbuds and said, "No gadgets at the table. You need to welcome our guest."

"What's Worser doing here?"

"We've invited him. And don't call him that."

"Why not? *She* calls him that," Seth said, and pointed at Donya.

Donya shrugged. "Everyone calls him that."

"That's awful," Mrs. Khoury said. "I'm sorry."

Worser wasn't sure what to say. He did hate his nickname, but early efforts to stop it had only made people more determined to use it, so he'd given up.

"Why do they call you that anyway?" Seth asked as he slid a piece of chicken onto his plate.

"Seth!" Mrs. Khoury flashed him a warning look.

"What? I want to know the story."

"It's not much of a story," Worser said. "On the first day of second grade, some ignoramus saw my name on a class roster. Everyone was listed by their first initial and last name, so, of course, mine was written as *W. Orser*. He read it out as 'Worser' to everyone, over and over. Apparently, they thought it was funny."

"Oh. I get it now." Seth took the salad bowl and dropped two tiny leaves onto his plate. "What's an ignoramus?"

"A stupid mean kid," Donya said.

"I know some of those," Seth said. "Anyway, I like Worser better than William. All the kids on my soccer team have nicknames. Rumble, Hopper, McFly, Booby Trap—although everyone calls him Boober. That one's worse than Worser. Ha! Worse than Worser."

"What's *your* nickname?" Donya asked.

Seth scowled. "I don't like it."

"Tell us. Tell us. Tell us," Donya chanted, lightly pounding the table with her fist.

Seth swung his elbow out sideways and whacked her arm. She thumped him on the back of the head. For some reason, they ended up smiling.

"Dude, come on. Worser told you the story behind his name. Tell us yours. It's only fair."

"Achilles," Seth mumbled into his lap. "Because I pulled my Achilles tendon that one time. I hate it."

Donya bumped shoulders with her brother. "Hey, the real Achilles was awesome. He was the strongest, most badass of all the Greek warriors."

"Donya. Language," Dr. Khoury said.

"I just meant," Donya restarted, rolling her eyes, "that Achilles was super strong. Practically invincible. You can work that angle, bro."

"Perhaps you can spell it differently," Worser said. "With a *k* instead of the *ch*, so it will have the word *kill* in it."

"Hey, I like that! And maybe a *z* on the end, because *z*'s are cool. A-kill-eez the Killer!" Seth pushed his chair away from the table, stood, and struck a muscleman pose. "Mom, I'm done. Can I go upstairs and do homework?"

Donya leaned in toward Worser. "In Seth-speak, *homework* means 'video games.'" She had never uttered anything in his ear before. The vibrations in her voice rumbled through him, fibrillating his heartbeat. By the time he'd recovered, Seth was already gone from the room. The others were quietly eating, oblivious to his cardiac event.

"Donya, what about you?" Mrs. Khoury asked. "How's everything?"

Dr. Khoury nodded. "Yes. How is school?"

"It sucks a million different things in a million different ways."

"Donya!" Mrs. Khoury glared at her daughter.

"Sorry. I was just illustrating my extreme disappointment through the use of metaphor."

"And hyperbole," Worser added.

Mrs. Khoury set down her knife and fork and looked pointedly at her daughter. "Perhaps you should explain?"

Donya began stabbing her chicken breast over and over with her fork. "Stupid Ludlum is going along with the district's stupid idea to cut librarians. Now Ms. Petrie is only on campus in the mornings and the library is closed after school. Lit Club lost its sponsor *and* its place to meet. Plus, there's no budget for the end-of-year magazine. I went to talk to Ludlum about it, and he said it wasn't a priority because there were so few students involved."

"Oh, honey." Mrs. Khoury reached across the table for Donya's hand, then seemed to change her mind and pulled it back. "I'm sorry about that. I really am. But what's done is done. Why not look at this as an opportunity to try something else?"

Dr. Khoury nodded again. "Yes. How about debate?"

"Stupid Hart is the sponsor, and he hates me. Says I'm too argumentative. Besides, I want to write."

"You could join the newspaper staff," Mrs. Khoury said, and glanced at her husband.

"Right." More nodding. "Or maybe yearbook?"

Donya shook her head so vehemently that her hair kept whacking Worser's shoulder—which he didn't mind at all. "No. No no no. I want to do creative writing. If I wanted to just lay out facts, I'd join Academic Decathlon again."

Worser had forgotten that Donya had been a part of that. She'd either quit or was asked to leave. Come to think of it, Donya did have problems with a lot of the school staff.

"There are still lots of creative things you can do at school," Mrs. Khoury said. "There's band and dance and..."

Donya was making a loud guttural sound and sliding down the back of her chair.

"Look," she said as soon as her mother was quiet again, "it's not going to happen, okay? Band and dance and orchestra and all those other things are full of people who've been doing it for years. I'm not going to suddenly take up violin and be playing 'Hot Cross Buns' next to some kid who's learning Paganini. Know what I've been doing for years? Writing poetry. And short stories. And flash fiction. I even have plans for novels."

Mrs. Khoury closed her eyes and rested her forehead on her fingertips—an expression that reminded Worser of Principal Ludlum's, although she wore it better. Meanwhile,

Dr. Khoury was employing Aunt Iris's favorite response: smiling weakly while shaking his head. Both reactions seemed designed to tolerate rather than to understand. Even though Worser would have used different syntax and a far less dramatic tone, he could relate to Donya's frustration. Budget cuts had also forced him from the library.

"Don't worry, my dear." Dr. Khoury smiled. "Perhaps you could start a literary club off campus. We have a binding machine at work, and I can cover the cost of the materials. Perhaps Mr. Ludlum will say it is okay for you to still distribute the magazine on campus. I'm sure it will all be fine."

Donya pushed her plate forward and slowly leaned over until her forehead was resting on the tablecloth. "No. No it won't," came her muffled voice. "Look, that's great and all. Thanks, Dad. But it doesn't solve the problem of a sponsor or where we can meet. Unless..." She glanced up. Her eyes hopeful. "The university wouldn't allow us to use a classroom, would they? That way we could just do the Lit Club on our own."

"Right. Well..." Dr. Khoury's smile lost its confidence. His nervous nodding restarted. "You see, I could get you in. But the others...the campus security checks..." Nod. Nod. Nod. "That would be difficult."

"You could meet at our house," Mrs. Khoury said.

"No. Never. The whole point is to do something away from home—ours or anybody else's in the club."

"What if your group found a location here in town?" Worser suggested.

Donya snorted. "Yeah, right. Like that's so easy."

"I might know of a place."

"Really?" She leaned toward him again. Worser felt a

swooping sensation, as if he were being tugged into her gravity. "Where?"

"There's a store selling used books not far from my house."

"A bookstore? In *this* town?"

"I know. I wasn't aware of it either until I came across it the other day. It has a big work table inside, and the guy who runs the place is, um, agreeable." Worser swallowed. "Anyway, perhaps we could ask him."

A curious thing was happening within Worser. As he sat at the table speaking to the girl of his dreams, he became aware of other voices inside him: thoughts he had pushed into the tiny, musty alcoves of his brain. They were wispy and remote—but menacing—and they were crying out like a horde of hellish dust bunnies. The more he talked to Donya, the louder their murmurings became until, finally, he heard them. *What do you think you're doing?* the bunnies cried. *Mr. Murray would never allow it. Even if he did, you'll lose your sanctuary. Stop!*

But Donya was looking right at him, her eyes shimmering so brightly that her fluorescent green hoodie faded from view. "Oh my gosh, I love you," she said.

And Worser heard nothing else for the next forty-five minutes.

Worser knew, in his main brain—that logical, unemotional, bunny-free part of his mind—that Donya had not actually been professing her love to him. And yet he couldn't stop replaying those words and remembering her sparkling gaze.

After he was dropped off back home, he spent several minutes on the porch, savoring the memory as he transitioned into new-home-life mode. The neighborhood was quiet. Weak light from the streetlamps strained through the half-dead hanging plants and cast shadow upon shadow, creating a mottled camouflage-like pattern on the wooden planks.

Once Donya's image began to fade, and the humidity of the still night air made him sweat, he headed inside. Fortunately, Aunt Iris was in the living room, playing music and probably working on her p-ohms, so she didn't hear him enter. Her interrogation would be delayed. Worser quietly set the plastic container of chicken Mrs. Khoury had given him in the refrigerator and headed to his mother's bedroom. On the way, he grabbed a magazine out of the basket where they'd begun storing mail and loose papers.

The study was dark, but his mother was still awake. The light from the hallway spilled in through the open door, revealing her wide-open eyes. She turned toward him. "Beh?"

"Hi, Mom." He stepped into the room, switched on the overhead light, and shut the door behind him. "Dr. Khoury says hello. He drove me back in their green Volvo. The one he calls The Frog—remember?"

He grinned, recalling their conversation after a visit to the Khoury house the year before. They'd found it so perplexing that anyone would name a car. Even so, it had inspired them to come up with possible names for their own old, rust-colored Nissan—The Log, The Cockroach, The Yam—eventually choosing, in a highly irregular fit of laughter, The Turd. It didn't catch on, of course, but it had been an interesting brainstorming exercise and an unforgettable memory. The two of them rarely had such silly exchanges.

Worser had hoped to make his mom smile, but she remained still and silent. Judging by the folds on her brow, she didn't remember or didn't find it amusing anymore.

No matter. He pushed aside a stack of folded clothes and settled into the chair next to her bed.

"How about I read to you? It's a short piece. I believe you'll find it quite entertaining." He held up the magazine. "Your journal arrived, and in it is a column reprinted from a major city newspaper—I forget which. The paper had asked area schoolteachers to submit examples of hilariously wrong answers to test questions."

Worser turned to the article and cleared his throat. "Here's one. Students had to use vocabulary words in a sentence, and one wrote 'The horse *precipitated* on the rocks.' Ha! Although I suppose that does demonstrate a crude understanding of the verb's meaning."

He glanced at his mother, searching for a reaction. If there had been one, he missed it.

"And this one is my personal favorite: A social studies teacher asked, 'Name three hardships the Pilgrims faced,' and one student wrote 'the *Niña*, the *Pinta*, and the *Santa Maria*.'" He burst out laughing. "Aren't you glad you teach college students?"

Her eyes fixed on his. She didn't seem confused, but she also didn't seem to find it funny.

This made no sense. She had grinned and laughed with Aunt Iris while they were dancing the other day, and his mother hated dancing.

"Beh?" She sounded sullen, like a toddler pouting after being denied a toy. "Beh?"

It was unnerving the way she stared at him—or *into* him, rather. The way she held her gaze so unabashedly. She had never looked at him in this way before the stroke happened. He didn't like it.

Worser averted his eyes and took note of the basket beside her bed, containing squeeze balls, a peg board, and other items she had been using to regain motor skills. The clock on the nightstand revealed it was nine fifteen. Suddenly it made sense: it wasn't that she didn't understand or appreciate his reading, she was just sleepy.

What a shame. He'd found the perfect thing to read to her and she was too tired to appreciate it.

"All right, I suppose that's enough for tonight." He grabbed the stuffed bear off the nearby table and tucked it under her arm. "Good night, Mom."

Right before he switched off the light and closed the door, he again noticed her eyes boring into him, as if searching for something.

For what?

He wasn't sure he'd ever find the answer. Even sadder, he wasn't sure he wanted to.

SEVEN

Appeal

The next Monday, at Re-Visions, Worser couldn't concentrate on his Masterwork entry. It was Labor Day, which meant no school, and, happily, the store was open—a dreamworthy set of circumstances. He'd even shown up an hour earlier than usual. But despite all that, he couldn't seem to shift into his usual highly charged, laser-focused frame of mind.

Because of his restlessness, he'd abandoned his chemical abbreviation words for something newer and, he hoped, more exciting: "Words That Can Transform into Other, Legitimate Words by Substituting Their Main Vowel with All of the Others (Except Y)." So far, he only had a list of six words—thirty, actually, if he were to count the different versions:

1. bag, beg, big, bog, bug
2. blander, blender, blinder, blonder, blunder
3. pat, pet, pit, pot, put
4. last, lest, list, lost, lust
5. mass, mess, miss, moss, muss
6. mate, mete, mite, mote, mute

He knew there had to be more, but it was difficult to think. He was too concerned about how to get Mr. Murray to allow the Lit Club to meet there. Now, in the harsh light of day, Worser understood how farfetched the idea had been.

There was something about Mr. Murray's disposition that reminded him of his mother—the way she truly was, as opposed to how she was now. Both had little tolerance for others' foibles and felt that idle chitchat was a waste of time. Both were no-nonsense, but she was brusque where he was crude. If they were fonts, she would be **Helvetica** and he would be `Courier`.

Despite his mastery of words, Worser knew he was unskilled at talking with people. He was also no good at flattery, which in this case wasn't a problem, since he felt certain Mr. Murray wouldn't be receptive to it. When he'd arrived that afternoon, he'd been so grateful to have a place to go, away from all the distractions of home, that he'd voiced his pleasure aloud. "Thank you again for the arrangement, Mr. Murray. This place is most impressive." To which, Mr. Murray had replied, without looking up from the novel he was reading, "Right. It's a regular Taj Mahal. It's a wonder they don't add it to the stops on the city tour."

He was sure that the best way to deal with Mr. Murray would be to come right out and ask him for the favor—and now was as good a time as any. Worser took one last look at his Masterwork pages, closed his binder, and rose from his seat.

Mr. Murray was perched on a stool behind the sales counter, hair as messy as always. He seemed lost in the paperback he was holding—what it was Worser couldn't tell, as the cover was bent back. Upon closer inspection, he noticed Mr.

Murray's lips moving, almost imperceptibly, while he read. Worser found this intriguing.

"Kid, what are you doing just standing there watching me? You're giving me the heebie-jeebies."

Worser could feel a substantial portion of himself turn and retreat. Before the rest could follow, he conjured the memory of Donya, smiling gratefully, and said, "Mr. Murray, would you be willing to host a small group of students once a week here in the store?"

Mr. Murray began one of his lengthy sighs.

"Allow me to explain," Worser said, hurrying on. "One of the students is the daughter of Dr. Khoury, a poetry professor, who could send his students here to buy books. Plus, they would all talk up the place to other potential customers. Before you know it, your store traffic would double. Perhaps triple."

"This is a group of college students?"

"Not exactly. I mean, not at all. They're in middle school."

"Just what I long for. A store full of teenyboppers. What a headache."

"It wouldn't be like that."

"Oh yeah? So, these bunch of nuisances, what are they like?"

Worser swallowed. It suddenly occurred to him that, other than Donya, he didn't know anyone in the group and couldn't vouch for their character. "They're very...literary."

"Literary," Mr. Murray repeated.

Worser had never heard the word uttered in such a way, as if it left a bitter taste in his mouth.

"Yeesh. Just what I need. A gang of pompous twits." He stared out the store's front window, his head starting to shake—subtly at first, slowly building in speed and size. "Look, kid, I—"

"Please, sir. Before you turn me down, allow me to add that . . . I'll do anything. I'm certain we could come up with a suitable agreement. Just don't say no."

"Kid, didn't you hear me before? Why do you have to keep calling me *sir?*"

"Just habit, I suppose. Probably the same impulse that causes you to keep calling me *kid.*"

Mr. Murray's feathery eyebrows raised up, and something resembling a smile washed over his face. "All right," he said. "Perhaps you have a point there." He stepped out from behind the counter and began pacing back and forth—again reminding Worser of a crested penguin.

After an unfathomable stretch of time, Mr. Murray stopped. "Okay," he said. "You want a deal? Here's a deal."

At this, Worser—who hadn't realized he'd been holding his breath—took an enormous gulp of oxygen.

"We keep our original arrangement. You make a purchase every time you come in—including for these meetings. But also, you'll come in on Saturday mornings for a couple of hours and help clear out that storage room in the back. It's full of all kinds of junk, maybe mice, too—something you should know if you're squeamish. Customers won't like it if they hear a bunch of screaming from the back room—and I know I won't."

"I'm not squeamish," Worser proclaimed—although, inwardly, he worried he might be.

"Fine. If you do that, and we agree that I can end the deal if these pals of yours wind up being a pain in my derriere, then I'll let them come in some evening during the week—any day except Mondays. Mondays are bad enough without me having to deal with a bunch of underage know-it-alls."

"How about Thursdays?"

"Sure. Whatever."

"Great. Um, could we have two hours?"

Mr. Murray looked so stone-faced that Worser worried the offer would be taken away.

Eventually the bookstore owner said, "Fine. You get from five to seven. That way kicking-out time is closing time. No hanging around after."

"Thank you."

"Sheesh. I must be getting soft in my old age."

When Worser arrived back home, he found both Aunt Iris and his mother in the kitchen. His mother sat at the table concentrating on spinning a yellow highlighter pen—one of her fine-motor skill exercises. Aunt Iris cheered her on while stirring something in a pot on the stove. Worser said his obligatory hellos and then tiptoed into the study.

Each time he entered the study, he somehow expected to find his mother sitting hunched over her desk, frowning down at whatever she was working on—even when he'd seen her just seconds before in the kitchen. Worser made his way to the desk, now shoved into a corner. He unearthed her old Rolodex from a teetering stack of files and flipped to the letter *K*. And there it was—*Prof. J. Khoury, poetry*—written in his mother's slanted cursive. He slid his fingertip over the writing, trying to imagine her making the entry. It looked as if she'd been in a hurry, but then she usually had been. He tried to envision his mother about fifteen years younger. A forty-something woman married to a sixty-something man, both soon to be older-than-average parents. Her first gray hairs appearing in her light brown hair. The crease between her brows beginning to permanently etch itself onto her face.

Worser hadn't made a phone call in a couple of years. He had vague recollections of calling up Aunt Iris as a very small boy to see if she could send him more of those chocolate cookies she'd mailed him (she could)—and once he'd called the public library to see if they could obtain a rare edition of Samuel Johnson's *Dictionary of the English Language* (they could not).

Worser lifted the card from the Rolodex, grabbed the phone receiver from its cradle, and sat on the ripped vinyl office chair, the gashes, he noted, now covered in multicolored Ging hair. He took a moment to silently rehearse what he would say, then balanced the card on his left leg, cleared his throat, and carefully punched in the number.

After a couple of rings, he heard Dr. Khoury's voice say, "Hello?"

"Hello, is Donya there, please?"

"No, she isn't. May I take a message?"

"Um..." Worser tried to recall the polite response. "No, you may not. Thank you. Goodbye."

That wasn't hard at all, he thought as he hung up the phone. He got up from the desk chair, then sat on the bed, roamed the small section of carpet between the desk and the door, and visualized Donya's hopeful, smiling face, until finally, after nearly half an hour, he decided to try again. This time, a different voice answered. Low refreshing tones, like the civilized hum of an air conditioner, belonging to the object of his affection.

"Hello," he said, his voice quavering, "is this Donya?"

"Worser? Is that you?"

"Yes. I have some news for you regarding the use of that location for Literary Club meetings. We discussed it at dinner at your house?"

"Yeah, yeah. I remember. What's the news?"

"I spoke to the proprietor of the bookstore, and he said it would be no problem. He suggests Thursdays from five to seven, if that would be all right with..." Worser trailed off.

Donya was no longer listening to him. Instead she was shouting *yes* over and over—at times a triumphant howl, other times a series of staccato *yes*es. The sounds were muffled, so she must have either dropped the phone or was holding it at arm's length. Her voice eventually returned to normal volume. "Sorry, I'm back."

"Was that a *yes* to Thursday evening? Or *yes* as a shout of jubilation?"

"Both. Yes to both. So Thursdays, then?"

"Right. From five to seven p.m. Will that work?"

"Perfect. I'll tell the others. Thanks so much. This was really great of you. I can't believe you went to all this trouble."

"I didn't mind going to all the trouble."

"Well, again, thanks. I'm sure I'll see you around."

"Yes. And I look forward to Thursday."

"Oh? You'll be there, too?"

Her pitch shifted ever so slightly. It made him tense.

"Yes..." Worser had never been good at lying, nor did he have much practice. But in that split second, before he was even conscious of the decision, he lied to Donya. "It was part of the arrangement," he told her, "since the proprietor already knows me and trusts me."

"I guess that makes sense. Well, if you're okay with it, I suppose I am, too. See you Thursday!"

"See you there."

Worser soon found himself in his room, sitting on the floor in his usual study spot. He couldn't recall hanging up the phone and coming upstairs, but he must have. He felt unnaturally light—as if filled with helium. His mouth remained in a soft, half-open smile as Donya's voice played on a loop in his mind. *See you Thursday!*

He would be able to spend two hours with her every week.

The fact made him so happy, he didn't even mind too much when he discovered a hair ball on his pillow.

EIGHT

Revealing

On Thursday morning, Worser woke up extra early. He was eager to get his day going so that it could speed toward 5:00 p.m.—when he would get to spend time with Donya at Re-Visions.

Over the past two days, he'd been trying to think up a scenario in which he could be her hero again, some gallant feat that would make her repeat the phrase *I love you*. But it was impossible to invent any such situations when all he saw of her were passing glances at school. He planned to spend this first meeting carefully observing—searching for ways he might prove himself invaluable.

Since he'd added his bookstore study sessions on Mondays and Wednesdays to the wall calendar, there hadn't been any repeat interrogations from Aunt Iris on his whereabouts. He'd hoped that his jotting down his newer, later return time on Thursdays after Lit Club would similarly appease her. But, alas, it was not to be.

"Seven-fifteen?" He heard her shout from the dining room as he finished up a bowl of cereal in the kitchen. A second later she appeared beside him, her face puckered with dismay. "Potato? I see you won't be home until seven-fifteen! What on earth has you out so late?"

"I have something important after school. It can't be helped." He spooned the last bit of flakes into his mouth and crunched as innocently as possible.

"I just don't understand. I expect big demands to be made on your time once you reach high school, but seventh grade? Kids today have far too much pressure on them, and it isn't healthy." Aunt Iris kept talking as she gathered items from various cabinets and drawers: a mixing bowl, a large spoon, measuring cups, salt, and a bag of flour. "I mean, honestly," she said, plunking the flour onto the counter. A faint cloud huffed from the bag, lightly obscuring her face. "Aren't you concerned that you're spending too much time studying? Maybe I should call that nice principal and complain."

Worser, after envisioning the call and another summons to the office, decided it might be more prudent to divulge the whole truth. "Actually, Thursdays are different from my after-school study sessions. I... I've joined a club."

Aunt Iris interrupted her baking to gape at him. "You *did*?"

"Yes. Literary Club. It meets every Thursday evening. At Re-Visions."

"I see. Well now. Good for you." His aunt looked so astonished and went so quiet that Worser seized the opportunity to head for the front door.

He'd taken three steps when she called out, "Wait!"

"What?"

"When can we go shopping for clothes? We still need to buy some for you."

"I object to the words *we* and *need* in that sentence."

"Didn't our misadventures last week when you were dressing for the dinner prove that to you?"

It had not, but Worser felt it would be unwise to say so.

"At least let me measure you." Aunt Iris picked up her tape measure and strode toward him, aiming for his waist.

In a single, fluid motion, Worser grabbed his backpack and rushed out of the house. He didn't stop hurrying until he'd reached the end of the block. By then, his pants were sagging below his hips because the elastic waist had surrendered, and his too-tight shirt was chafing at his armpits.

As the panic wore off, the aggravation set in. It irked him that his aunt was so determined to mother him. The woman was forty-eight years old and had no life—just two insane cats and a junk-building business she referred to as "art." He couldn't wait for his mother to get strong enough and verbal enough to tell her sister to move back to her herbal-scented apartment. Then everything could go back to normal.

Better than normal. Because thanks to the club, he'd be spending two hours a week with Donya. Starting today.

At school, the hours passed like a billowy cloud on a day with no wind. Often, Worser found himself sitting in class, grinning to no one in particular. When he wasn't in a Donya-inspired reverie, he was checking the time and wondering if Principal Ludlum could have secretly paid someone to make the building's clocks run more slowly. He knew that was improbable, and yet he was continually surprised to find that only a moment or two had passed since he'd last checked.

So Worser waited and huffed and daydreamed and shifted in his seat. An entire archaeological period rose and fell into history. Eventually, the final bell rang. Worser said a quick goodbye to Herbie—who was pondering aloud whether human whiskers could work the same as cats' if they grew outward and long enough—and raced toward Re-Visions.

By the time he reached the shopping center, his feet hurt and sweat stains spotted his faded polo, making it chafe even more. He wanted some sustenance, but was too nervous to eat, so he drank two large Gulpees from the U-Bag'M.

It was still a half an hour before meeting time when the bells over the door announced his entrance into the bookstore. He paced in a small oval, intermittently wiping the sweat from his upper lip. His stomach was a flooded basement.

After using the bathroom and checking his appearance in the murky mirror above the sink, he was demoralized to discover, via the electronic clock on the cash register, that only five minutes had passed. This was definitive proof that time was relative, and the day's slower pace was caused by his own heightened perception—as the thought of Mr. Ludlum and Mr. Murray being in cahoots defied all logic.

Worser considered writing in his Masterwork, but he was too nervous to sit. He could only manage more pacing, which turned into a bouncing dance as his bladder refilled.

"May I use the bathroom?"

"Again?" Mr. Murray eyed him suspiciously.

"It's because I drank two—"

"Kid, please. I don't need to know the details. Sheesh." He held up his hand in a halt gesture. "What's with you? How come you can't keep still?"

"I'm just eager for the meeting to start."

"The bookworm meeting you talked me into." He shook his head. "You're a real mover and shaker, aren't you, kid?"

Worser had to agree, as he was doing lots of moving and shaking.

When he returned from the bathroom, Mr. Murray gave a five-minute homily on the definition of public restroom and how the closet-sized bathroom in the store did not meet it. He then said Worser should relieve himself at home on Thursdays and show up at the store closer to meeting time. Worried that Mr. Murray might change his mind about their arrangement, Worser agreed.

All this lecturing managed to pass the time, but it also made Worser need to pee yet again. As he was making his third return trip, Donya walked through the door.

"This is so great!" she said, looking around. She headed for the counter and grinned at Mr. Murray. "Thanks for letting us meet here."

"Don't mention it," Mr. Murray replied—which would be a very polite reply from anyone else, but Worser was fairly sure he'd meant it literally.

Donya didn't seem to notice. She wandered about the store, her beautiful brown eyes wide with amazement.

Worser's gaze followed her until she disappeared around a nearby bookcase. When he faced front again, he saw Mr. Murray squinting at him.

"Now it makes sense," Mr. Murray said.

"What makes sense?"

"Nothing. Go help the lady and leave me alone."

Once the other students had arrived, Donya began the meeting by saying, "I met with Principal Ludlum this morning and explained that we are going to continue the Literary Club off campus. Even though we will no longer be a school club, he has allowed me to hang a large envelope next to the library doors so that people can submit items for consideration for the magazine. Mr. Ludlum agreed to have the info mentioned during morning announcements, and there'll be a notice in the school newspaper. He also said once we have all the material for the magazine, he'll read it, and if he approves, we can distribute it on campus. The envelope is supposed to stay up all year, so if you see that it's missing, tell me. Or tell Mr. Ludlum. And tell him he's a clueless jackass who has no business helping to mold the minds of young people."

Worser smiled. It was apparent that Donya was the club's leader, which made him feel proud for some reason. He'd never seen her in action like this—all chutzpah, spunk, and pluck. Donya was made of words with pop and sizzle. Like fire.

He had settled into an extra chair along the wall rather than at the table. Worser typically avoided social settings, but if he had to be in one, he far preferred to watch interactions from an aloof vantage point rather than take part in them. Like a spy. Or Jane Goodall observing her chimpanzees.

Despite the safety of his location and the thrill of being in Donya's presence, he felt a strange uneasiness—only he wasn't sure why. Immediately after sitting down, he got the distinct sensation that something was amiss. He wondered if he'd just gotten used to sitting at the oak table, with all its pockmarks and ink stains, and whether he'd feel better if he were there. But the only empty seat would have put him to Donya's right, with a tall person between them. Here he could gaze at her without anyone's head in the way. He relished this view of her, standing in command at the far end of the table with the rest of the group in dim profile.

Mae Kim sat at Donya's left. Worser couldn't recall when

he'd learned of the existence of Mae—sometime after he started middle school. Like Donya, she was as cool and tough as an all-honors-class-taking student could be, but gloomier and less talkative. Mae was famous for her spiky magenta hair, five shades of eyeshadow, T-shirts with snarky sayings (today's was NOT MY CIRCUS, NOT MY MONKEYS), and black Doc Martens boots that, last year, had famously kicked the crotch of a loudmouthed high schooler who'd called Mae and her girlfriend a heinous and unoriginal slur.

"I wouldn't hold your breath," Mae said. "Last year's magazine had only Lit Club members' stuff in it. Why should this year be any different? We're the only people in school who care about creative writing."

"Except for the English teachers!" said Felicity Redfearn, who sat on Mae's other side.

Mae regarded her for a couple of seconds. "I stand by my statement," she said.

"Well, I'll have you know that Mrs. Sansom was reading to us from *The Book Thief*, and she cried."

"Probably because the state just gutted her retirement."

"You!" Felicity wrinkled her nose and tittered. It was, Worser thought, a textbook example of the word *titter*—high-pitched, trilling, and birdlike. Mae winced and Mr. Murray's "Sheesh" could be heard from across the store.

Worser recognized Felicity from his algebra class. Her incessant chatter, always punctuated with squeaks and giggles, had made her known to him. She was the kind of person who added an extra *eee* sound to the end of *hi* or *bye*. The personification of the word *bubbly*—right down to his imagining her drifting off into the sky, never to be seen again. He wondered if Aunt Iris had been like this as a girl.

"Can we go ahead and share our stuff?" asked Lee Ontiveros, the obstruction on Donya's right. Because he was male and chummy with Donya, Worser had been scrutinizing this club member the most.

"Not yet," Donya said. "Be patient, Lee."

Lee: one weak consonant and two repetitive vowels. Worser shuddered at the thought of Felicity pronouncing it. And yet it fit him. Lee was as slight as his name. Tall, but not imposing, and curved inward at the shoulders like a walking question mark. He had long thin legs, a long thin ponytail, and a moldy-looking fuzz on the tip of his chin.

"Before we start, I want to acknowledge someone." Donya looked right at Worser and smiled. It was so lovely and unexpected, he had to look down. And that was when he discovered why he had felt odd: His pants zipper was gaping open.

He quickly moved his hands over the gap.

"Worser arranged with Re-Visions to let us use this space," Donya went on. "We should all give him our thanks."

Worser dared to glance up again when he heard the applause. Everyone was grinning at him. If they had caught a glimpse of his not-quite-white briefs, it didn't show in their expressions.

"You should come sit with us." Felicity gestured to the chair across from her.

Worser shook his head.

Felicity's grin faltered. "'K," she said with a quick shrug. A few seconds of awkward silence followed. Then everyone looked back at Donya.

"All right. I shall now start off our sharing with my latest work in progress. It's a poem, called 'Ludlum, the Mop-Headed Half-Wit.'" Donya shook some stray hairs away from her face, cleared her throat, and read out loud:

> Your annoying voice
> Too much tremolo
> Like a freshly neutered Schnauzer
> Your skinny upturned nose
> Nostrils like hairy quotation marks
> Announcing your disdain
> Someday
> I'll punch it.

Again, the group burst into applause. Worser enjoyed the spirit of the poem (even if the word choice was lacking in places) and very much wanted to join in—but he dared not move his hands.

"Thoughts?" Donya asked.

Mae gave her a thumbs-up, Felicity said something about Schnauzers being cute, and Lee said he loved the part about the nose best of all. Donya glanced at Worser, but he remained in position, completely silent.

He knew he had to fix his pants. But first he needed for everyone to be facing away.

"Me next!" Felicity said, her right hand shooting toward the ceiling.

Worser's groan was drowned by Felicity's pushing back her chair. Felicity was closest to him. Now he'd be in the background as everyone watched her.

"This is a haiku called 'Butterfly.'" Standing very straight, she regarded everyone with a pert grin—glancing back to include Worser—and began to recite:

> I see light yellow
> Buttercup petals flutter
> And take to the sky.

Felicity made a noise like *hee!* and plopped back down into her chair. While her tablemates applauded, she giggled and pushed at the air in front of her, as if being tickled by invisible hands.

"That," Mae said, "is so you."

"Thank you!" Felicity said.

"All right, Lee," Donya said. "Your turn."

"Finally." Lee said it, but Worser thought it. With all eyes focused on Lee, he could at last see to his dilemma.

For the next few minutes, Lee shared the latest pages of his work in progress. Worser was too intent on zipping back up to pay close attention, but he could tell from the phrases that did penetrate his skull that the story was a high fantasy, involving elves who communicated with their minds. Apparently, Lee also intended the tale to be illustrated, as he would pause now and then in his reading to hold up drawings.

Meanwhile, Worser's zipper kept sticking, making progress slow and difficult. By the time Lee finished, Worser was only halfway zipped.

"Okay," Donya said. "Thoughts?"

"I liked it," Felicity said. "I especially like Seldor. I love that he has a pet squirrel."

"Nikiki isn't his pet—it's his familiar," Lee said. "Their spirits are intertwined."

"What's your page count up to?" Mae asked.

"With illustrations? Two hundred sixty-five," he said. "And a half."

"Dude! And you're still introducing characters?" Mae slapped a hand to her forehead. "I mean, I'm no expert, but shouldn't they be on their quest by now?"

Lee made a scoffing sound. "This is an epic adventure that will span several books. I need to set up the story correctly before they begin their journey; otherwise, readers will be confused."

"Yeah, well, you're assuming readers will stick around."

"At least I actually wrote something instead of just talking about it."

"I'll share when I'm ready!"

As Mae and Lee bickered, Worser decided to close his fly the rest of the way. His mistake was in thinking the disagreement would continue verbally, rather than segue into silent glares.

"Did you just hear a zipper?" Felicity was glancing his direction. The others followed her gaze.

"It's...my bag." Worser leaned over, unzipped his backpack, and grabbed his notebook. "I was removing an item from my bag."

"Wow. Did you actually bring something to share?" Donya asked.

Worser paused. "Um..." He wasn't sure what she meant by *actually*.

Through some superhuman feat of speed or time travel, Felicity was already out of her chair and standing at his side. "Ooh. Masterwork? I like the sound of that. What is it?"

"It's a project I've been working on for a few years."

Now everyone was craning to see his binder.

"That also looks like a couple hundred pages," Mae noted. "I hope your story has an actual plot."

"It's not a story," Worser corrected. "It's a lexicon."

"Lexicon," Felicity repeated. "Isn't that one of the beasts in your book, Lee?"

Lee shook his head. "I think it's a geometric shape."

"A lexicon is a reference book on language—a study of words and how they are used," Donya said, and Worser's heart seemed to sprout wings and fly loops inside his chest.

"Cool!" Felicity exclaimed.

"Why are you writing a lexicon?" Mae asked.

"I..." Worser faltered. Now all eyes were upon him. How did this happen? He was here to gaze at Donya, not to be gazed at. "I wanted to."

Felicity was now bouncing on her toes. "Can we see?"

"Maybe you could just read us part of it?" Donya asked.

Worser didn't want to reveal his project. Only his mother knew of its existence. Over the years, he'd shared a handful of pages with her—ones he knew she'd enjoy and not be too critical of. The rest he wasn't sure about.

The mere thought of reading from his lexicon made him feel vulnerable and exposed. Like letting someone see him in his underwear—something he'd literally avoided only a moment before.

But Donya. The way she regarded him right now, with keen interest and surprise—it was like food he didn't realize he needed.

Slowly and tenderly, he opened his binder and flipped the pages. He scanned the entry titles, hoping to find something—anything—to make Donya smile.

"Words That Sound Scary"? No. Too subjective.

"Words That Exemplify Their Meaning"? No. Too woefully incomplete. So far, he only had *multisyllabic*, *lilting*, and *assonance*.

"Words You Can Pronounce Correctly with Your Mouth Open"? No. Too embarrassing to read aloud.

Flip, no. Flip, no. No. No. No. No.

Ah. This one might suffice.

"Here's a sampling," he said. His voice came out reedy and a half pitch higher than normal. "The title of the entry is 'False Antonyms.' This is what I have written…

"As the prefix *de-* means 'off' or 'from' and typically negates its root, confusion could result with several English words. For example, *debunk* sounds as if it means 'to get out of bed.' *Denote* and *describe* should mean 'to erase.' *Descent* should be synonymous with *deodorize*." Worser glanced up. "It goes on from there."

The Literary Club was staring at him. Donya's furrowed brow was a clear sign that he'd disappointed her.

"I should mention that I wrote this entry when I was much younger," he added. "On a day when I was feeling uncharacteristically facetious."

"That"—Mae pointed at the binder in his hands—"is super cool."

Lee nodded. "Really interesting."

Felicity started clapping. "Oh my god! I love it! That's so true about the words. I used to think *devoid* meant 'to fill something up,' but it actually means the opposite. So confusing!"

Worser was both excited at Felicity's comment and chagrined that he hadn't made the same observation himself.

"You've got pages and pages of this kind of stuff?" Donya asked. The note of awe in her voice made Worser feel as if his whole body were lifting and protracting—a sunflower seeking her nourishing rays.

"I have several other entries," he said. "Most aren't so frivolous, but I do enjoy good wordplay—if it's done right."

"Did you include *detail* on your list?" Mae asked. "It sorta sounds like what lizards do if you pick them up."

Donya laughed. "Right? And I always thought *deluxe* sounded like it meant '*less* fancy.'"

Worser joined them at the table, and for the next hour, the members of the Literary Club helped him add to his entry. He was pleasantly surprised at their suggestions, and astonished that they also enjoyed such mental exercises.

By the time the meeting had ended and the group moved to the front of the store, Worser had added a new page to his binder—a bonus list of dictionary definitions for false antonyms beginning with *de-*.

delay (v)—to stand up.
demean (v)—to become a kinder, more generous person.
define (v)—to reimburse a penalty fee.
decoy (n)—someone who is less shy than they used to be.
deride (v)—to hop off a bicycle or skateboard.
defile (v)—to scatter important papers.

Lee had wanted to add an entry for *depot* (verb—to plant back into the ground) but was denied since the *t* was silent—a ruling he and Mae were still arguing about as they headed out of the store toward their parents' cars.

"Omigosh, that was so much fun we're so going to do it

again, right?" Felicity said to Worser as she fastened the chin strap on her bicycle helmet.

Her delivery was so rapid-fire that it took him a moment to process.

By the time he opened his mouth to respond, she was already skipping out the door, calling, "Okay, see you later, bye-ee!"

Felicity's departure returned the store to its usual level of quiet—a loud quiet that seemed full of something. Promise, perhaps?

A few feet away stood Donya, grinning at him as she zipped up her hoodie.

"That..." She paused and shook her head. "That was seriously the best meeting we've ever had. How did I not know you were creating a lexicon?"

"Probably because we don't interact that often, and you rarely ask questions of me."

Donya's features twisted into an indecipherable expression. She glanced down at the floor and said, "Yeah."

A car horn sounded. Worser peered through the window and saw Dr. Khoury pulling The Frog up to the curb.

"Ah. Transportation awaits," Donya said as she shouldered her messenger bag. She had just put her hand on the metal door handle when she paused and looked back at him. "Hey, Worser? I never said this before, but I should have. I'm really sorry about what happened to your mom."

With that, Donya quickly pushed through the door and jogged to the Volvo. She didn't notice that the skin around Worser's eyes had turned a subtle shade of pink, like the inside of a seashell. She didn't see his lips purse, his eyes blink rapidly, or his too-tight shirt strain with his jagged breath.

But Mr. Murray did. He was looking right at him when Worser turned around.

Worser took a moment to stuff his emotions into a metaphorical suitcase and toss it into a metaphorical closet. Then he trotted back to the oak table and began returning the chairs to their pre-meeting positions.

"Hey, kid." Mr. Murray appeared beside the bookcase. "Leave it, will you? I got this."

"I don't mind," Worser said. "Besides, I promised to tidy up after."

"Forget it. You'll probably do it wrong anyway. Just go home, will you?"

Worser froze with worry. "Mr. Murray? Are you not satisfied with our arrangement?"

Mr. Murray rubbed his whiskers. "That tall guy needs to buy better deodorant. And the loony one with the braids? Eesh. That laugh of hers made my spine pucker. But overall, I have to say it was...tolerable."

"So, our agreement still stands? Our group can continue to meet here on a weekly basis?"

"Just don't forget about Saturday. You promised to start cleaning out the storage room, and I'm going to hold you to that." Mr. Murray waved his hand toward the door. "Now get out of here, will you? Go home before you can't recognize your family anymore."

NINE

Reflection

Sitting across from Aunt Iris at breakfast the next morning, Worser stared down at his toast. It struck him as familiar, in a vaguely painful way. Shifting uncomfortably in his chair, he yanked the waistband of his slacks down a couple of inches to make room for his protruding belly. That's when it came to him: the light beige of the bread was the same color as yesterday's peekaboo underwear.

It was time to surrender.

"I've decided you may have a point about my needing new garments," he announced.

Aunt Iris's eyes widened from behind her teacup. She swallowed and said, with a bit of a gasp, "I'm glad to hear it. What brought about this change of mind?"

Worser hesitated. "It doesn't matter. The point is, I shall allow you to purchase me new clothes."

"Hooray." His aunt's tone didn't quite match her response. "How about today right after school? I'll see if I can get Ms. Lucretia to sit with your mom. Constance will be tired from her sessions and probably just sleep the whole time. If I can arrange it, I'll call the school and get a message to you. Sound good?"

"Fine." He stood and pushed his chair under the table.

"Have you said goodbye to your mother?"

"I attempted to, but she was still asleep." This was a half-truth. He had peeked in through the partially open door and saw her lying in bed—although he couldn't say for certain she was asleep. Again, he'd been struck by the foreignness of her. Her grown-out hair was beginning to show Aunt Iris–like waves. Her facial features, while familiar, were held at new angles. Even her stare, when he allowed himself to meet it, revealed something different behind her eyes. Or perhaps what was different was the willingness to reveal anything at all.

He thought of Mr. Murray's parting quip: *Go home before you can't recognize your family anymore.* His mother was his mother—only she wasn't. Meanwhile his aunt was behaving like a mother. Or, rather, a smother.

No one was who they should be.

The school day unfolded as usual, but with a few noteworthy exceptions. Mae Kim waved to him as he stood in the student center, waiting for Herbie to arrive. Felicity approached his desk before algebra class and pitched him a false definition for *decompose*—although the sonics of her speech left him unable to follow it.

The best part of all was seeing Donya in the hallway between second and third period. She grinned at him as she approached and then, just as they passed each other, called out, "Hey." It had been worth the resulting stumble into a water fountain.

At lunch, Worser sat with Herbie in their usual spot in the cafeteria—a far corner where the custodians lined up the full rolling rubber trash cans beside the service exit. It wasn't the best-smelling section of the cafeteria, but it was the quietest and offered the best view. Here, he could eat in relative safety, keep an eye out for Donya and any approaching tormentors, and routinely wonder why someone felt it necessary to stamp the word INEDIBLE on the side of every trash can. He couldn't imagine anyone mistaking a trash can for a vending machine.

As usual, Herbie sat opposite him. Both boys straddled the tiny, saddle-shaped perches the cafeteria tables offered as seating. This was another design Worser often pondered. On the one hand, because they were attached to the tables, the seats cut down on noise and disarray. But whoever invented them must have been four feet high and naturally cushiony in their private regions. Thankfully, lunch always ended before key body parts went numb.

Today, Herbie kept squirming in his seat. He appeared to be contemplating his worn Converse sneakers. In order to see his shoes, Herbie had to completely extend his legs—almost tripping two unsuspecting sixth graders a few minutes earlier.

"My shoes are too tight again, so Nanna's driving us to the mall after school to get me new sneakers," Herbie said.

"Why go all the way out to the mall? There are several department stores here in town. In fact"—Worser paused for a noisy sigh—"I'll be in one of them this afternoon. It has been revealed that I need new clothes."

"We have to go the mall. I need a special shoe size, and none of the stores around here carry it." Herbie regarded his feet again.

"Well, I'm sorry. Malls are dreadful."

"I don't mind them. I just wish we didn't have to go so far. Long drives make me nervous."

Worser frowned. "Why?"

"It's just…" Herbie drew his legs back and leaned forward, resting his elbows on the table. "If you get in a car accident while picking your nose, do you think your finger could go up through your sinus cavity, into your brain, and kill you?"

Worser stared down at his slab of cafeteria meatloaf—grayish brown with tiny chunks of red and green—and pushed his tray aside. It was one of those times when he wondered if eating lunch as a loner outcast would be preferable to eating with Herbie. Yet, as usual, he couldn't help puzzling over the question. "I highly doubt that is something that occurs. At least, not often."

"But you've got to figure the impact would at least cause your finger to rip your nostril open. Right?"

Worser shuddered. "Perhaps you should just make sure you never pick your nose while riding in a car."

"I'll try. But, you know, sometimes it just happens."

Worser managed a nod. There were some things about which Herbie was wise.

He again considered the chunks in his meatloaf. Something about the shade of green called up visions of Donya's hoodie. This got him thinking about Donya, which reminded him of his deal with Mr. Murray to clear out the back room. At the time of the agreement, he'd been too relieved to fully consider it, but now he worried about holding up his end of the bargain. His experience with hard labor consisted of carrying a backpack to and from school.

He studied his tall lunchmate. Herbie was wiry but had large, shovel-like hands that matched his feet.

Worser straightened up and cleared his throat. "Herbie, I require some assistance."

"From me?"

"Yes. I need help tomorrow clearing out a friend's storage room."

"Wow."

Herbie's response confused Worser. "I recognize that it doesn't sound enjoyable."

"No. It's just...we've never hung out together before—in real life."

This was a statement of fact. However, Worser wasn't sure why it was uttered in amazement. He began to worry that Herbie would say no. "If you assist me, I'll treat you to food afterward."

"Like at a restaurant?"

Worser thought of the U-Bag'M, the only business in the shopping center that served anything edible. "More like fast food."

"Okay. Sure." Herbie's curls bounced as he nodded. "Speaking of treats, I'm going to get one of those chocolate-dipped ice cream cones. Want one?"

"No, thank you."

Since Herbie was being so obliging, he decided not to tell him that he boycotted the ice cream station on principle—annoyed at the brutalized words painted on the freezer's exterior, like ICEE! and TASTEE! It reminded him of Felicity and her overemphasis on the long *e* sound. (Perhaps she spelled her own name *Felicitee?*)

While Worser brooded, a familiar shape passed in front

of him. It was the man-boy, Turk, loping down the aisle on the other side of the table. Their eyes met, briefly. Turk did a double take, pivoted, and pointed both index fingers at him.

"I know you?" he said.

It was an ineffective way to word a question.

"We spoke briefly outside the locked doors of the library," Worser replied.

He watched Turk consider this. It appeared that squinting helped him process things mentally.

"Right." Turk's features relaxed. "Library Boy. I remember. So, what are you doing here?"

Worser paused, wondering if Turk was playing him for a joke. "I'm eating lunch," he said, deciding the question had been sincere.

"Here?"

It was one of the most incomprehensible conversations Worser had ever had. "Yes."

Turk shook his head. "So much suckage. You should sneak off campus." He lifted a crumpled, orange-striped bag that came from the burger restaurant across the street.

"I..." Stunned as he was that Turk was talking with him—again—Worser didn't think it wise to mention his strategy of avoiding potential bullies and their lairs. "I can't risk it. The principal has already been targeting me."

Again, Turk's head shook pityingly. "Successive," he said, which made no sense whatsoever. Then he took the crushed bag, balled it up even more, and pitched it into one of the nearby trash cans.

"Hasta huevo," he said—which Worser was pretty sure translated into more nonsense—and loped away.

❖❖❖

Worser stared at himself in the full-length mirror on the wall beside the dressing rooms. He was wearing a button-down shirt with a purple pattern on it that reminded him of microbes. He would confess to knowing little about fashion, but it seemed to him that people would want to avoid looking like a walking petri dish.

"Now that looks smart on you," said Aunt Iris's reflection as she came up behind him.

"Intelligence has nothing to do with appearance."

"It's just an expression. So, what do you think of the shirt?"

"It's discordant. I prefer clothing that isn't headache-inducing."

"Try this." She handed him a green crew-neck tee with two thin bands of blue across the front, along with a pair of black jeans.

Both items fit, and he found nothing to object to—beyond his having to put them on.

Aunt Iris applauded when he emerged from the dressing room. "Very nice."

He did the "stress tests" for her, which involved sitting down, raising his arms, and bending over to see if anything strained or came unbuttoned. He turned to inspect his backside. He assessed whether the fabric itched. While he had to admit these examinations seemed sensible, they also heightened his humiliation. The stress tests were, indeed, stressful.

Worser wondered why so many people enjoyed clothes shopping. During the twenty-three minutes they'd been at the store, Aunt Iris had lectured him on several rules of style. He was instructed never to mix patterns, educated on the difference between "warm" colors and "cool" colors, and told that red tones washed out people with his complexion.

"My. That shirt really makes your eyes pop," his aunt commented.

"Sounds violent."

"Plus, green is such a soothing color. It will heighten your sense of self-love."

"What poppycock. Clothes are supposed to keep you covered and protected from the elements. That's it. Everything else is trivial and shallow."

"Oh, don't be such a sourpuss. Clothes are a way of expressing who you are." Aunt Iris lifted her left arm with a flourish, accentuating the bell-shaped sleeves of her magenta top. Her various metal bracelets made a jingling sound as they slid together near her elbow.

Perhaps there was something to what she was saying. After all, Aunt Iris was loud—in her laugh, in her speech, and in the bold colors she always wore. Even her jewelry rattled and jangled. In a truly literal sense, her purple-and-red wardrobe suggested she was elaborate, excessive, and possibly communist.

"So, how about I find you more green-colored tops for you to try on?"

Worser pondered the shirt he had on. Green was the color of the outdoors and was a synonym for *park* and *eco-friendly*. It could also mean "unripe," "immature," "envious," or "naïve." He did not want to be known as green.

"No. Just the one will do."

"You know"—Aunt Iris tilted her head and squinted at his reflection—"you should wear more soft blues, since you're a summer."

"I'm a what?"

"A summer," she repeated, heading toward a nearby rack. "That's your palette."

Worser had already learned that he was a boys' L/XL or a men's medium who needed the "hefty" trouser cut. Now he'd learned he was a season—and his least favorite one at that. No wonder he felt sweaty and fatigued.

"What about this one?" She picked something off a nearby rack and held it high: a sky-blue Henley with puffy navy-and-white letters that read POWELL.

"Why would anyone purchase a shirt that has someone else's name on it?"

Aunt Iris shrugged. "Some people are very brand-conscious. There's no Orser line as far as I know."

"That is not my point. I wouldn't even wear something that had my own name emblazoned across the front in such a garish way. Is it too much to ask for a simple, solid-colored, unadulterated shirt?"

"We'll find you something. Never fear."

"I'm not afraid."

He could hear his own petulance. How he bent the last word of each sentence into a lower pitch, the way his breath came out in haughty puffs. While he couldn't argue that the outing was a waste of time, he also didn't want his aunt to assume this was fun for him—or that he was overly grateful for her help. He told himself that his mother would be doing this with him if she could. Of course, another part of him—the smallest, most interior nesting doll—whispered that that probably wasn't true. When he and his mother had shopped it was only when they absolutely had to—and they had always raced through the process. It's possible now that he was in seventh grade that she might have just handed him a bus schedule and wished him luck. But even so, he would not let Aunt Iris take over his affairs the way she'd taken over their house. This was a one-time event.

Aunt Iris continued flipping through the contents of the circular clothes rack. "We should also get you a sweato or two while we're here. Cool weather will be upon us before we know it."

"Sweato?" Worser repeated. "What on earth are you saying?"

"I'm doing you! Oh, you had the cutest lisp when you were little. All your *l*'s and *r*'s were *w* sounds, and anything that ended in *-er*, you pronounced as an *o*. 'I want to weah my sweato.' So adorable!"

"I have no idea what you are talking about."

"Oh, come on. Surely Constance told you."

"Never."

"That's a pity."

"No, it isn't. What would be the point?"

Aunt Iris didn't seem to hear him or, perhaps more likely, was ignoring him. After finishing her inspection of the clothes rack, she threw up her hands and shrugged in that overly dramatic way of hers. "No plain, soft blue sweaters that I see. Most of the blues are dark," she said. "It will be different when we come back next spring for some warm-weather clothes."

That's when Worser's protestations, his breath, his movements came to a stop. Aunt Iris had said *when we come back next spring*, as if it were an inarguable fact—which meant she felt she would still be living with them, and that his mother would not yet be recovered.

It was a thought that had not occurred to him, a dreadful

one. Like so many other things, his aunt was probably mistaken. After all, if she referred to colors as seasons, she obviously had a distorted sense of time.

"Oh, look. This is plain," Aunt Iris said, handing him a black turtleneck. "And this coat would look very nice on you." She thrust a light tan jacket at him. Still in shock and too distracted to object, he returned to the dressing room and put on both items.

"Now, see? That's one way to express personality," she said when he'd emerged to stand in front of the mirror. "Here. Try this hat, too."

Before he could balk, Worser found himself wearing a black knit beanie.

Worser finally pulled himself out of his thoughts enough to focus, and he decided he looked ridiculous. Taken together, the black cap, black pants, and black turtleneck poking out of the ill-fitting jacket combined to make him look like a bolded, lowercase *i*. For *irrational, ignominy, intimidation*.

"Oh my. Don't you look dapper! Like a beatnik. They were wordsmiths, too, you know."

"Charlatans on hallucinogens."

If Aunt Iris had heard him, she gave no reaction. She swiveled the cap around on his head, looking for the perfect tilt as she studied him in the mirror.

"I've noticed you haven't gone in to read to your mother these past few days."

Worser, who was still recovering from her talk of springtime shopping, was caught off guard. He stared down at the gray industrial carpeting. "I've had a great deal of homework."

"I know it's upsetting to see her like this. No one blames you. But your visits in the evenings are such a comfort to her."

"You don't know that." Worser frowned at the reflection of his aunt's face hovering over his own. "She gives no indication that she's enjoying my readings. She's probably too tired. You wear her out with all of your childish activities."

"You don't need to read to her. Just be with her. Just be."

"You use that phrase constantly, and it is meaningless. How can I not 'just be'? What, specifically, are you saying I should do with her?"

"Nothing!"

Counting Turk's babbling at lunch, this was Worser's second pointless conversation of the day, and his patience was as frayed as the shirt he'd worn to the store. "You are making no sense at all!"

"All I'm saying is that you don't have to do anything or say anything. Just be near her. Listen to her."

"Listen to her?" He spun around and glared at his aunt. "Are you trying to be funny?"

Aunt Iris had sense enough to look contrite. "I mean, listen with your heart, not your ears."

"The vital organ that sits behind my rib cage, whose main function is to pump blood through my body? You want me to somehow use that to decipher my mother's limited speech?"

"You are being too literal. I am talking about opening up your heart."

"Which would cause all cardiac activity to cease and would prevent me from 'just being,' as you keep telling me to do."

"Oh, Potato. I don't want to debate semantics with you. I just want everyone to be happy. That's all." She took the hat off his head and placed it back on the peg. "What do you want?"

What did he want? Worser stared at his sullen expression

in the mirror. He wanted to go back to before his mother's stroke, that's what.

No. That wasn't it. He wanted to speed forward—to a time when his mother didn't need Aunt Iris anymore, and neither did he. To when their home could again be a cat-free, paint-fume-free haven. To evenings when his mother would upbraid him on his word choice and list all the ways the English language was being abused as she read the paper. He wanted to rid himself of the feeling that he had walked through this looking glass, like a character in the novel by that Victorian deviant.

That was what he wanted.

Instead, he said, "Well, I don't want this absurd outfit. Can we please just find some basic clothes? Quiet and normal. That's what I want."

TEN

Trip

"Are you wearing that today?" Aunt Iris asked as Worser walked into the kitchen the next morning.

Worser glanced down at the yellow Henley and charcoal jeans he had on—one of the three outfits he had deemed acceptable enough for his aunt to purchase for him. "Is that a rhetorical question?"

"But we just bought those."

"I fail to see your point. Did we not purchase them for me to wear?"

"Your new clothes are for school. I kept some of your old clothes, the ones that weren't falling apart, for you to romp around in on weekends."

Worser scoffed. She made it sound as if he'd be frolicking in a field. "I shall not be *romping*." He picked up one of his aunt's scones—which he always translated to *stones* in his head, for the way they sat in his stomach.

"Besides," she went on, setting her empty teacup in the sink, "I need to wash those new clothes."

"That's lunacy. Why would they need to be washed when we just bought them?" As was often the case since Aunt Iris came to stay with them, Worser found himself stuck between two thoughts—either his aunt knew nothing, or he didn't. And considering this was his home, he felt his side should carry more weight.

"They put chemicals on the garments so that they keep better, and those can give you a rash. Plus"—she reached out and snatched a hair off his shirt, making him jump—"there's cat fur covering it already. You really need to hang up your clothes or keep them folded in drawers so that the cats won't be able to reach them."

Worser considered launching a counterargument, emphasizing the need for Aunt Iris's pets to be better trained or, preferably, reintroduced to the wild outdoors, where they clearly wished to be. But he was supposed to meet Herbie in twenty minutes at the bookstore, and it would be faster to simply change.

On his way to the staircase, he passed his mother shuffling out of the study. She was draped in a scarf his aunt had purchased for her yesterday—lime green with a pink-and-blue floral pattern. And tassels! It looked... wrong, almost criminally so, like graffiti on a national monument. Aunt Iris should have to pay a fine and do community service.

"Good morning, Mom," he said.

The left side of her mouth turned upward. "Bah." She was still focusing on *b* sounds in her therapy and *Bah* was new—although she still often asked for the bear.

"I'm afraid I'm running late," he said as he continued up the stairs. "I'll try to come read to you later, but I have a lot of stuff to do today, so I might not—" Worser broke off. His foot was not landing where he needed it to. At the exact second, a multicolored blur streaked through his peripheral vision, and

Worser found himself falling forward. His knees came down on one step, hands on two others. The half-eaten scone sailed out of sight.

His mother lurched toward him, making a series of sharp sounds. Behind her, he could see Ging—no longer in motion, but still hazy from her fur standing on end. Both the cat and his mother wore matching startled expressions.

"I'm all right," he said, scrambling to his feet. "See?" He extended his limbs and made exaggerated flopping motions. "Not injured."

He ran the rest of the way upstairs, panting in anger at Ging, his aunt, and the law of gravity—but unable to vent aloud.

Because he was certain he'd deserved it.

"Mr. Murray, this is Herbie."

Herbie nodded, as if agreeing. "Hi."

Mr. Murray peered at Herbie over the cover of his paperback. "Huh. Are you another one of them?"

"Another one of them what?"

"Herbie is an associate of mine from school," Worser explained. "He has volunteered to help me work in the storage room today."

"Oh yeah?" Mr. Murray's bushy eyebrows flew to the top of his forehead. He leaned toward Herbie, studying him closely. "Why would you do a thing like that?"

"It sounds like fun."

Mr. Murray looked even more skeptical.

"There was also the promise of snacks," Worser added.

"You're a regular Tom Sawyer, aren't you?" he said to Worser. "Whatever. As long as the job gets done."

"Whoa." Herbie was now facing the opposite direction, his head turning in a wide circle as he gazed up and down the nearby shelves. "This place is great. Do you have any Kurt Vonnegut?"

"Do I look like a card catalog?"

"What's a card catalog?"

"Eh, forget it. If you can find it, you can buy it. Just don't expect me to fetch it for you. Now let's get to work."

The boys waited as Mr. Murray locked the front door and turned the BACK IN 15 MINUTES sign so that it was facing out. Then he led them behind the sales counter and down the tiny hallway marked EMPLOYEES ONLY. To the right was the small bathroom. Opposite that was another door. Mr. Murray opened it.

As the fluorescent lights flickered on, Worser's determination morphed into doubt. The space was far larger than he'd expected, filled with boxes and bins, some stacked in towers taller than he was. The musty scent of the storage room was far less pleasing than the bookstore's. It reeked of decay rather than age, of putrefaction rather than petrification. He didn't mind clutter or mess, and he had grown accustomed to the fetid smells of his own room, but this was different. His mind began formulating sentences that would relieve him of this promise, but before he could utter them, he thought of Donya and her sweet goodbye to him two nights earlier. The memory repowered his resolve.

"All right. Here's what I need you fellas to do," Mr. Murray said. "This room is full of both stock and junk. The only way to tell the difference is to go through each of these boxes and assess the contents. If the books are filthy, ripped, warped, or missing parts of their covers, they are junk. Pages should be as near to white as possible. It's okay if they've turned a little yellow as long as the structure of the book is sound. But if the paper is the color of morning pee, they are junk. If they are not even books, they are junk. Junk should be put in the boxes over there," he pointed across the room, "right by the back door, so they can be more easily removed from the premises. Stuff that isn't junk goes in these." He gestured to the plastic bins beside him. "Got it?"

Worser raised his hand.

"Sheesh. What is it?"

"Mr. Murray, if we come across a rodent, should we call for you?'

"Do I look like an exterminator?"

Worser had no idea how to reply to that.

"Not my problem, kid. If it happens, deal with it yourself. Just no shrieking, okay? You guys need to keep things quiet."

"We will," Worser promised.

"And don't lift anything heavy. Empty the big boxes before you move stuff around. I don't want anybody to get hurt."

"That's nice of you," Herbie said.

"Just avoiding lawsuits, kid. Don't read too much into it." He glanced down at a large silver watch on his left wrist. "It's almost ten-thirty now, so what say you stop at twelve-thirty? I can't have you here all day."

"Okay." Herbie lifted his arm. "I have a watch, too. It has an alarm that I use to wake up in the mornings and remind me to brush my teeth. I'll set it."

"You do that. Well, then. Best of luck to you, fellas." Mr. Murray headed back into the store, leaving Worser and Herbie to blink at each other amid the boxy landscape.

"Wow, it's humid in here," Herbie said, pulling at the collar of his T-shirt.

Worser nodded. "Agreed. Nothing *mid* about it. It would be more precise to say *hu-max*."

He had hoped Herbie might chuckle, but all he got in reply was a solemn nod. Wiping his forearm across his brow, Worser made a mental note to wear lighter "rompwear" the next week. "Well, I suppose we should get started."

"Okay." Herbie sat on the floor and pulled a nearby box toward him. "Nanna made a really good breakfast this morning. She thinks I do better with more protein, so today she made me migas. Ha! That's fun to say."

Made me migas. Worser had to say it himself and found that it was, indeed, enjoyable the way one's lips bounced with the consecutive *m* sounds. He wondered when his mother might be able to say it. Would she also find it entertaining?

The work wasn't difficult, but it wasn't enjoyable, either. As Herbie's prattle began to become indistinguishable from the hum of outdoor traffic, Worser found himself pondering his situation.

Weekends used to be the most precious of his days. With no school for him and no classes at the university for his mother, they would spend hours in various semireclining positions on the living room's sofas and armchairs. Mostly, she would grade papers while he wrote in his Masterwork, but there were also books, puzzles, the occasional game of Scrabble, and—even rarer—trips to an unassuming restaurant for dinner.

Without fail, there would be wordplay—puns and other zingers that slipped into their conversation like pepper chunks in their entrées. "We can order the duck, if you don't mind splitting the *bill*," his mother would say while perusing the menu at their favorite eatery (preferred for its service, silence, and decorum). "No waffling. I'm definitely having pancakes," he'd announce at the diner. Once, they picked up dinner to go at their second-favorite eatery and had been delayed on the way home by roadwork. What began as complaints about their food growing cold turned into a series of clever quips. "I can't wait to eat my en*chill*adas!" "I'm looking forward to my *brrrrito!*"

Remembering those times brought on a squeezing sensation behind Worser's ribs (which also could have been where the scone-stone half had lodged). It was disorienting to realize how different things were now.

But there was also Donya. That had changed, too—for the better. By focusing on her, on what was right instead of wrong, he could stop the dark, downward-tugging feelings and keep working. He continued this way until a high-pitched beeping snapped him out of his reverie.

"Oh, hey," Herbie said, swatting at his watch. "It's twelve-thirty. Can't believe it's been two hours already. Want to go get snacks?"

"Sure," Worser said as he staggered to his feet. His arms and back ached, sweat had pooled in crevices he usually wasn't aware of, and the dust was making his head feel stuffy. It felt as if he'd evaluated thousands of books, and yet, to show for it, there was only one large box of rejects near the back door and one medium-sized plastic bin of possible stock beside the other door. Thankfully, the only vermin he'd come across were dead insects.

Herbie, who worked much faster, had filled a larger bin with possible stock and two large boxes of recyclables. He had also found a pack of gum—a stick of which he'd tried and found too tough to chew. "Maybe it's fossilized," he'd said as he stuck the pack in his pocket.

Worser had worried that Herbie would object to receiving his edible payment at a convenience store. But when Worser mentioned the U-Bag'M, Herbie seemed excited.

"You two look like feral dogs," Mr. Murray said as they emerged from the storage room.

Worser glanced at Herbie. Dark patches covered his exposed skin where grime had adhered to the sweat, and his curly hair had somehow increased in diameter. He imagined he must be similarly disheveled, the main difference being (besides their ectomorph versus endomorph body frames) that Herbie was grinning.

"We're going for food at the U-Bag'M," Herbie said to Mr. Murray as they walked around the sales counter. "Want us to bring you back a corny dog?"

"No thanks. I don't live that dangerously, kid."

"We did as much as we could in the allotted time," Worser said.

"I'm sure you two will pick up the pace next week," Mr. Murray said.

At the words *you two*, Worser glanced nervously at Herbie—who had only committed to helping this particular day. To his astonishment, Herbie was nodding.

"Yep," Herbie said. "We'll go faster next time."

Worser stood in place, flabbergasted that Herbie would sign on for such a task, and unable to decide if this raised or lowered his opinion of his friend.

His lengthy pause seemed to annoy Mr. Murray.

"All right. Get going. I know I'll see you soon enough, kid," he said to Worser. He then glanced at Herbie. "You I'll see next Saturday. Unless you'll be here Thursday with all the other brainboxes?"

Herbie looked confused. "What happens on Thursday?"

"Mr. Murray allows the Literary Club to meet here," Worser explained.

"Oh. Cool. Yep, I'll see you Thursday, Mr. Murray," Herbie said, heading for the exit.

"Whoopee."

Worser trotted to catch up with Herbie. "Wait. You want to come to the Literary Club meetings?"

"Sure," Herbie replied, and stepped out into the sunshine.

On their walk to the U-Bag'M, Worser tried to come up with reasons why Herbie shouldn't join Lit Club—but couldn't. It wasn't that he didn't want him there, only that it felt precarious to add one more element to the situation.

After one Gulpee drink, two off-brand beef jerky sticks, and a Snickers bar, he still hadn't come up with any genuine objections. Moreover, he couldn't ignore the fact that Herbie had spent the morning helping him with a filthy, laborious task and was now agreeing to do it on a regular basis. For these reasons alone, Worser decided that Herbie joining Lit Club was a good idea. If not good, at least harmless.

Which was more than he could say about the beef jerky.

Even when he didn't have a stomachache, Worser hated being in grocery stores. They were an assault on his senses. Too crowded, too noisy, and too packed with useless, garish commercial items with wince-inducing puns in their names. (Although, he had to admit to a fondness for Marz-Mellows!—a star-shaped, Day-Glo breakfast cereal that his mother accidentally bought on a hurried trip.)

Yet here he was. Three seconds after he'd arrived home from his outing with Herbie—tired, sore, and wishing he'd chosen better food options that day—his aunt had swirled into view. She announced that they'd all be going shopping, that they were out of key provisions, that his mother needed to get out of the house, and wouldn't that be fun?

Worser had said no, it wouldn't, but that didn't make Aunt Iris alter her plans. So far, his answer had been proved right.

"Potato," his aunt said as she inspected a large apple, "could you please go grab some baby arugula?"

"This is bewildering. It is unreasonable to have so many different variations of a green-leaf vegetable. No wonder this planet is in trouble. Why not just have one or two and give over farmland to something else—like libraries?"

"Well, why do we have to have so many words that mean 'confused'? *Puzzled, perplexed, bewildered*... Why not just say *confused* and get rid of the rest?"

Worser's mouth fell open. He shut it and inhaled through flared nostrils. "Because," he said, trying to control the angry waver in his voice. "Because there are differences, sometimes significant and sometimes subtle, and it's useful to have a wide range of choices to fit various contexts. Besides, there's the matter of personal taste. I myself prefer *baffled*, as it sounds more like its meaning. And *bumfuzzled* is a regional synonym I'm partial to—although some people think it sounds like an obscenity."

"Well, greens are probably that way, too. There are subtle differences, and different people prefer different ones."

Worser felt as if he'd sauntered right into a trap. But rather than argue and add to the length of their outing, he trotted to the lettuce section and found the redundant vegetation Aunt Iris had requested.

On his way back to their cart, he saw that his mother and aunt were laughing. Not just laughing but giggling. He felt that familiar stinging sensation up the back of his neck, along with an urge to flee—both responses intensified by being in a public place. His mind sought the perfect word for his emotional state: *aggravated? exasperated?* The closer he came, the more he could pick up the lingering scent of sandalwood that accompanied his aunt everywhere. *Incensed*—yes, that was it.

"What are you two doing?" he demanded.

"Constance is petting a kiwi."

"Why are you putting her up to this?"

"Up to what?"

"Fondling fruit!"

"Don't be silly."

Worser fumed at the accusation that he was the one being silly when the two of them were patting a piece of produce as if it were a gerbil.

"Constance likes how fuzzy it is."

"You don't know that."

"Just look at her. Look at her laugh."

Worser didn't want to behold the image of his mother, with her lopsided grin, letting out high-pitched hoots as she cradled the kiwi between her palms.

Meanwhile, Aunt Iris was doing her own chirruping laugh. "It does tickle," she said. "Here, feel it."

"No! You're going to get us thrown out."

If he were to be honest with himself, being ordered to leave was not what concerned him, as he didn't want to be there to begin with. What he truly objected to was Aunt Iris continually taking advantage of his mother's weakened state to include her in harebrained antics. The whole scene was demeaning, and if his mother had been well, she would have agreed. She was above all this clowning about.

"Oh, you." Aunt Iris's non-kiwi-holding hand dismissed him with a wave. "We're just having a bit of fun."

Fun? Fun to his mother was a Sunday *New York Times* crossword puzzle or a game of Scrabble with added rules. Petting an oversized berry? This was *not* an Orser form of amusement.

As it turned out, the feeling of being on exhibition proved to be accurate. A young woman was standing a few feet away, watching them. Worser couldn't tell if she was charmed or shocked by this display of juvenile behavior. She took a few tentative steps toward them, paused, pressed her lips together, and then closed the gap between them in three brisk strides.

"Dr. Orser?" she said to his mother.

His mother glanced at her. He couldn't tell if she recognized the young woman or not.

"Hi," the woman said. "It's good to see you."

For a few seconds the two of them stood smiling and bobbing their heads at each other.

"She was my professor," the woman said to Aunt Iris. "She was tough, but I learned so much. I was sorry to hear about what happened to her."

At that precise second, Worser came to understand why *snap* was a synonym for losing one's temper, because he heard an actual snapping sound in his head. Before he realized what was happening, words were pushing their way out of him.

"Why are you talking to *her*," he said, gesturing toward his aunt, "when *she's* here?" He pointed to his mother. "*She's* right here in front of you. Don't act like she can't hear you."

Over and over he jabbed his finger toward his mother. He wasn't yelling, but a roar-like rumble had crept into his voice. "Don't pretend she's not here. Don't assume she—" He broke off. It suddenly occurred to him that he, too, was referring to his mother in the third person. His fury instantly turned to shame.

"I...I'm sorry," the woman said. She took a couple of steps backward, then turned and hurried away.

His mom and aunt were looking at him. Neither was smiling anymore.

"That was incredibly rude," his aunt said.

"Why do people do that?" he asked, staring down at his shoes. "Why do they use the past tense when talking about her, as if she died?"

His aunt didn't reply. He heard a rustle of scarves and smelled her exotic fragrance. Soon a hand was on his shoulder.

Worser pushed it off with an exaggerated shrug. "I'll be in the car," he said, and headed toward the welcoming EXIT sign.

ELEVEN

Perfect

"Everyone, please give a warm welcome to..." Donya faltered. "Sorry. What's your name again?"

"Herbie."

"Everyone, welcome Herbie."

The rest of the Lit Club members uttered *hi* or *hey* in unison. Herbie smiled and nodded at each of them.

"Did you bring any writing to share with us?" Donya asked.

Herbie continued to nod. "I brought a book."

"You wrote a whole book!" Felicity exclaimed.

"No." Herbie looked confused. "It's by Octavia Butler."

Donya exchanged an incredulous look with Mae. "I meant, did you bring any of *your* writing. We typically share stuff we created."

"Oh. Then no."

"Okay, then." Donya shuffled the papers in front of her.

This week, Worser had the seat immediately to Donya's right as she sat presiding over the meeting from one end of the table. In fact, he'd arrived early so that he could claim the chair before anyone else. Lee, who had nabbed the favored spot last time, sat to his right, directly across from Herbie.

Meanwhile, Mae sat opposite him, and Felicity sat at the other end of the table.

Just as he had during dinner at the Khourys' house, he felt hyperaware of the nearness of Donya, captivated by every detail and movement. For a change, she had taken off her hoodie, and Worser found himself transfixed by the downy hair on her arms. She looked so soft—almost sueded. He wondered what it would be like to give her a gentle pat.

The reddish hairs on his own arm looked thicker and stiffer than hers. He doubted his would have the same feel, but tried it anyway, stroking the fleshy part above his elbow. It was surprisingly soft to the touch. Her arm would undoubtedly be softer.

"Are you cold?"

Worser jumped at the sound of Donya's voice. "Um, no," he replied. He let go of his arm and clasped his hands together tightly.

Donya turned back toward the group. "So the only thing in the submission envelope this week was a Twix wrapper."

"At least it's *something*," Felicity said. "Maybe things are getting better."

"Yeah, maybe next week they'll include the candy bar," Mae muttered. Today she was wearing a T-shirt that read HANDY HUMAN INSIDE—JUST ADD COFFEE.

"Oh, ha!" Felicity brushed her braids over her shoulders. "I just mean, it's good that people are noticing the envelope."

"Let's get down to official business," Donya said, pounding her fist against the table like a gavel.

"How does this work?" Herbie asked. "Do you have an agenda?"

Mae snorted. "An evil agenda."

Pearson and the Duwamish Longhouse and Cultural Center. The story poles in the book are fictional, but they are inspired by real story poles carved by the Duwamish artist Michael Halady. Learn more and support at: **duwamishtribe.org/longhouse**.

To Jasmine Warga and Lauren Magaziner, for offering the exact right notes at the exact right time; to Booki and Lauren, for the retreats, group texts, love, and support; to Jake Arlow, for the writing dates—you are all gems.

To my parents and siblings—for reading drafts, for offering wisdom, for making me who I am—I am unendingly grateful to you.

And to Josh, always. Your commitment to making the world a better place inspires me every day. I don't know what the future looks like, but I'm glad I get to discover it with you. I wrote this poem in refrigerator magnets the year we moved to Seattle, the year I started this book. It was a reminder every morning as I wrote, a love poem for you, for our city, for a moment in time. If this book has a heartbeat, it's this.

If this is calamity,
I will spend it with you
in this city we love
& not drive
but watch the sun kiss the highway
and the ships dream of sea

One Tree Planted is an environmental nonprofit dedicated to global reforestation. Since 2014, they have planted 171 million trees with 489 partners across 84 countries—and made 112 cities greener by planting urban trees.

Learn more at **onetreeplanted.org**.

"Nothing super strict," Donya said. "But we usually open with everyone sharing new compositions. So, who wants to go first?"

"I'll go," Lee said.

Lee's latest writing comprised three new pages of his fantasy epic. It involved Seldor meeting a couple of new characters, Branwen and Ghislane, two elven princess warriors who were described in lengthy detail. As he read, Mae gave feedback in the form of resting her forehead on the table and fake snoring. Lee ignored Mae, finished narrating, and held up intricate drawings he'd made of the elven princesses.

"Pretty!" Felicity said.

"Very nice," Herbie said.

"How come all of the females in your world have big boobs?' Mae asked.

"Rhea doesn't."

"She's an owl."

"Well, she's female."

"Face it, dude. You like drawing boobs."

Lee's brows lowered so dramatically, they almost covered his eyes. "That is not constructive feedback."

Mae snorted. "Why isn't it?"

"It's more of an observation," Worser cut in. "A constructive comment would be if you said he needed to draw smaller boobs, or bigger boobs, or—"

"Can we stop talking about boobs!" Donya threw up her hands.

From the front of the store, Mr. Murray muttered something like "Cheese and crackers."

Donya pressed her lips together and took a slow breath. "Any other feedback?"

Herbie raised his hand.

Donya and the others looked as surprised as Worser felt. "Yes?" she said.

"You said the elves were vegetarian," Herbie said to Lee.

"They are," Lee said in an authoritative tone. "They befriend all animals and refuse to eat them."

"Huh." Herbie looked confused. "So why do they wear leather breeches?"

"Because..." Lee trailed off and sat silent for a moment while the others exchanged glances. "They only use the leather when they find the animal already dead," he concluded. "And then give them a ceremonial burial, of course—after getting the leather."

"Oh. I see," Herbie said, seemingly satisfied.

"Let's move on." Donya rifled through the pages in front of her, accidentally brushing her elbow against Worser's forearm. The resulting touch felt only slightly weaker than a Taser stun. "Who else wants to share?"

Nobody said a word.

"Seriously? That can't be everything. We still have..." Donya checked her phone, "an hour and a half left. We can't end the meeting this soon."

Felicity let out an excited gasp and raised her left hand. "I know! Maybe we could play a game?"

"Like what?"

Felicity spun about in her chair. "Excuse me, Mr. Murray?" she shouted through cupped hands. "Do you have any games?"

"Does this look like a toy store?"

"I think he means no," Felicity said with a shrug.

"Well, we could always read." Donya glanced at the nearby shelves. "Or just...go home, I guess."

The wounded note in her voice was almost too much for Worser to bear.

"Actually," he said. "I might know some games."

"Sorry, Herbie. The correct answer is"—Worser paused for effect—"*pulchritudinous.*"

They were finishing round three of a game he used to play with his mom called Spot the Impostor, in which a person tries to decide which of three words is genuine.

"Pulchri-what-a-what? That's for real?"

"*Pulchritudinous,*" Donya said. "I actually knew that one. It means 'ravishingly beautiful.'"

Lee snorted. "*Pulchritudinous?* No way."

"Your disbelief is reasonable," Worser said. "I agree that the word sounds nothing like its meaning. A shame, but they can't all be perfect words."

"Wait," Mae said, holding up a hand. "You think some words are perfect?"

"Yes."

"Like what?" Felicity asked.

Worser glanced around the table. They were all pivoting toward him expectantly. "Well... like *lift.*"

Donya cocked her head. "How is *lift* perfect?"

"Just look at it. It evokes its meaning with its upward appearance. All of its letters are tall and thin. The word *thin* is almost perfect—but for the *n.*"

"Neat!" Felicity said, with an enthusiastic toss of her braids. "What else is perfect?"

"The word *bed.*"

"*Bed?*" Lee asked. "How is that perfect?"

Worser wrote out the word. "In lowercase, the word looks

like a bed. With the back of the *b* and *d* resembling a headboard and footboard."

"Huh." Donya turned the word into a chuckle. "Never thought of that."

"What else?" Felicity asked, bouncing in her chair.

"*Galoshes*," Worser said.

Felicity wrinkled her button nose. "How does *galoshes* look like its meaning?

"It doesn't. But it's full of wet sounds, and has a walking rhythm to it, so it evokes its meaning that way."

The rest of the group began saying the word *galoshes* aloud, over and over. Worser couldn't help but smile. He'd never believed there were other people his age who might appreciate all this.

"So, *galoshes* is onomatopoeia?" Lee asked.

"Not technically. It doesn't imitate sounds on purpose—like *hiss* or *bark*. It comes from the singular *galoche*, which is a Middle English word for a type of shoe. Its perfection comes by chance."

"Have you ever noticed that sometimes names are that way?" Herbie said. "Like the poet whose last name was Wordsworth? And that super-fast runner guy whose last name is Bolt? And I have a neighbor whose last name is Brewer who makes beer in his garage."

"Is this list of perfect words in your Masterwork?" Felicity asked.

Worser shook his head. "It isn't. But perhaps it should be."

"It should be!" Felicity exclaimed. "And we can add to it!"

The game was abandoned, and for the next twelve minutes, the group nominated the following list of words that might be deemed "perfect":

- *Squiggly* has lots of squiggly letters.
- *Bump* has lots of bumps.
- *Kink* has two kinked *k*s in it. (Mae preferred *kinky* because it also contained an angular *y* at the end, and Worser reluctantly agreed that she had a point.)
- *Wavy* is wavy, if written in cursive.
- *Hoop* and *loop* are nearly perfect with their double *o*'s and the round part of their *p*'s.
- And *awkward*, with its *k* trapped between two *w*'s, looks rather awkward.

"I've never really thought about words being perfect," Donya said.

"Me neither," Mae said. "I mean, I have favorite words, but that's just because I like how they sound."

"Ooh! What are they?" Felicity asked.

Mae sat hunched, avoiding eye contact. Worser had never seen her look bashful before. "Okay fine. I have four: *talisman, gossamer, evanescent,* and *cellophane.*"

"Those are pretty!" Felicity clapped her hands together. "You know, I always liked *bumblebee*. And *September*. It's the most beautiful-sounding month. No offense, Mae."

"None taken."

"I would have to disagree with you," Worser said. "To me *September* is evocative of many revolting words, like *septic* and *sepsis*."

Felicity lifted her chin. "Well, I think it's pretty. Just like *chandelier*—which might be the loveliest word of all."

"I always liked *bungalow*," Lee said. "Ever since I was a kid." He glanced at Worser, as if worried he might object.

Worser said nothing. He had to agree it had a nice bounce to it.

"I like *serendipity*," Donya said.

Soon they were compiling a list of favorite words on a piece of notebook paper Lee produced:

cellophane, talisman, gossamer, evanescent, September, chandelier, bungalow, serendipity, serenade, sashay, chagrin, penumbra, soiree, promenade, summery, bliss, moonbeam, crystal, melody, eloquence, Camelot, credenza, taffeta, bibliophile, parfait, glimmer, icicles, lingerie, sumptuous, clementine, dulcet, ballerina, lagoon, poetry, amber, dragonfly, ingenue, ephemeral, Chantilly lace, mauve, kerfuffle, grenadine, canoodle, phosphorescence, pomegranate, pom-poms, tresses, elixir, grace, dalliance, crêpes suzette, epoch, minuet, shimmy, chassis, darling, ethereal, murmur, pageant, moment, syzygy

"What about you, Worser?" Felicity asked. "You haven't added any words yet. Do you have a favorite-sounding word?"

Worser opened his mouth, then hesitated. He was about to shake his head, but there was something about the way all five of them were staring at him—expectantly, trustingly—that bolstered him.

"I always liked *mother*."

Half an hour later, a red-faced and slightly breathless Mr. Murray dashed around the nearby bookcase. "What's the matter back here?"

He gestured toward Felicity, who was laughing—hard. She had turned the deep pink of a Valentine's Day card and was jerking backward in her chair. The noises emanating from her mouth and echoing throughout the store were her usual titters, only much louder, each round kicked off with the ear-piercing shriek of a bird of prey.

"What the hell happened?" Mr. Murray pressed again. "What's wrong with the screechy one?"

Mae shrugged. "I don't know. All I said was *panties*."

This set off another shrill sequence from Felicity. "It's just funny," she gasped. "You saying *panties*."

"Sheesh!" Mr. Murray tugged at his hair on both sides of his head. "I thought someone was having a fit. I almost called the paramedics."

"Sorry," Donya said. "We'll keep it down. Things just... got a little out of hand."

"We're making a list of words we can't stand to go along with our list of favorite words," Herbie explained.

"Are there any words you dislike?" Mae asked Mr. Murray.

"Plenty."

"Maybe you can help us," Donya said, smiling the kind of smile that typically placates adults. "So far, we just have *squirt, dollop, moist, glom*, and, um"—she gestured to Felicity—"what she's laughing about."

"Is there a word you hate most of all, Mr. Murray?" Herbie asked.

Mr. Murray stared up at the ceiling. His already grimacing face bunched up even more. "*Ointment*."

The entire table cracked up. Even Worser felt a laugh bubble up, which surprised him.

"Ah." Mr. Murray raised his hand in a dismissive wave and began trudging back to the counter. "Just wait till you're my age. You'll see."

"Hey, guys." Donya glanced down at her phone. "Let's pack up. We only have about five minutes left. So...next week. Don't forget to bring new stuff to read."

Worser remained at the table as the others peeled off, one by one.

Felicity gathered up her things, strapped on her bicycle helmet, and headed for the front door, all while muttering, "*Syzygy. Syzygy.* Hee!"

Next, Lee and Mae left, with Mae teasing Lee about *boobs* being a perfect word. "Just look at those two *o*'s, side by side."

Lee let out a grunt. "Can we not?"

Herbie followed close behind them, saying over his shoulder, "I have to meet Nanna at the U-Bag'M, since she can see it more easily from the road. If I hurry, I can get a Gulpee before she gets there. Bye!"

Worser gave a wave, which Herbie didn't see. Soon, the bells on the door signaled Herbie's exit, and once again the room filled with meaning and possibility.

Donya got up and began slipping on her hoodie. Worser stood and slowly zipped up his backpack, trying to match her pace. Together they headed to the front of the store.

"You know," Donya said, shouldering her bag, "I'm really glad you joined our group." Worser grinned softly, choosing to ignore the surprise in her tone. "If it weren't for you and your games, this meeting could have been such a bust."

He wondered if she was making a pun after all the talk of boobs, but her smile seemed sincere.

"These meetings are fun." Worser shuddered at his basic declarative sentence. It was shockingly difficult to find the right words to express the relief mixed with exhilaration mixed with gratification that Lit Club gave him. He'd have to invent a new vocabulary.

Donya smiled wryly. "I know what you mean." She turned to stare out the front window at the darkening day. "This is about the only time I can stand this provincial town."

It was one of her regular refrains, one that baffled Worser. "Why do you dislike our town? It's got an educated populace, low unemployment, reasonable taxes, highly rated schools—"

"All right, all right. Don't get me wrong—I think it's a great place to be *from*," Donya said. "It's just not a great place to be."

"I fail to see the logic in that sentence."

"What I mean is..." Donya's mouth bunched up, and her brown eyes gazed toward the ceiling.

Her expression was a textbook example of *deliberation*, and Worser adored it. *D* for Donya, plus *liberation*. He wondered if losing herself in deep thoughts was the only time she felt free.

"Look," she said eventually, "Oak Valley isn't the Ninth Circle of Hell or anything—it just doesn't have what I need."

"What's that?"

"Variety. Don't you get tired of always doing the same things with the same people in the same places?"

"No." On the contrary. Worser mourned the loss of sameness in his life: that easy, expected routine with his mom before she fell ill. The comfort it had given him.

He'd taken it for granted before. He wouldn't make that mistake again.

Donya's brow furrowed. She seemed to be reading him. "How's your mom doing?"

"She's...working hard. She moves better and can do

things like dress herself and brush her teeth. I'm hoping she'll be back to normal soon." The topic triggered the usual feelings of restlessness for the future, and he paused to steady his breath. "That's all I can tell you. It's hard to adequately evaluate her recovery when I'm not a doctor."

"That's fair. I guess I didn't necessarily want a detailed health assessment. I just wanted to show that I care."

A honk sounded.

"There's Dad. Need a ride?"

"No. I need to make a purchase."

"Okay. Hey..." Donya reached out and touched his arm—in the same spot he'd touched just an hour earlier. "Thanks again for your help."

She was out the door before he could respond, which he was incapable of doing anyway. Worser was stunned, in all senses of the word—both pleasantly bewildered and not fully conscious. Eventually, he shuffled to a nearby bookcase, pulled the first book he saw off its shelf, and ambled toward the sales counter. As he moved, he was aware of a warm, tingling sensation on his arm where she'd touched him. A delightful branding. A magnificent sunburn.

"Don't worry about it for today, kid. Put the book back," Mr. Murray said.

"But it was part of our arrangement. I agreed I would buy—"

"I said don't worry about it today."

Worser hesitated.

"Ah, jeez." Mr. Murray said, when Worser wouldn't budge. "Look, the short, frowny one with the disco hair bought a bunch of Anne Rice books before the meeting started. We're all good here, at least for this time."

"Okay. Thanks."

"Meh." Mr. Murray waved his comment away.

Worser headed out of the bookstore feeling changed. It was a mood he hadn't experienced in quite a while. He pondered the right word as he headed home.

Cheerful?

That wasn't right. *Cheerful* involved a big grin, and he wasn't wearing one. But he did feel lifted and light.

Pleased was a teacher who had elicited a correct answer. *Merry* was an inebriated person singing holiday songs while wearing an outlandish hat.

There was only one other word that could be right. A word he wouldn't have thought possible—especially since his mother's illness.

Happy.

TWELVE

Belongings

The feeling Worser termed *happy* lasted through the following four weeks.

He didn't object much when his aunt organized the hall bathroom and threw out anything she deemed "not bathroom-related"—including an advanced crossword puzzle he'd been working on intermittently for two months.

He wasn't bothered at lunch when Herbie saw shapes in his chicken nuggets. "A T. rex! South America! A chicken? Hey—a chicken nugget shaped like a chicken!"

He even entered into an unspoken détente with Aunt Iris's cats. Instead of growling, hissing, and attacking Worser's bare feet, Seer had taken to merely pinning back his ears in a look of utmost annoyance whenever he saw Worser. Likewise, Ging was showing herself more often, eyeing him warily from behind furniture or the opposite ends of rooms.

Meanwhile, he made such good progress on his Masterwork during his solo bookstore hours that the corners of his mouth were getting chapped from his tongue-tapping habit. He'd also had to add paper to his binder, the bulk of which was putting more strain on the front seam. He knew he should get around to starting a new one—a volume two of his Masterwork—but he liked seeing all the pages together, the visual evidence of his hard work.

He and Herbie finished cleaning out the storage room at Re-Visions. It was larger and nicer now. A raised platform had been buried under the boxes, and they had also found a stack of wooden folding chairs, a tinsel Christmas tree, and a battered old Spider-Man comic that Mr. Murray let Herbie keep. All that remained in the room were three plastic bins of "to keep" items, the chairs, and a mound of Bubble Wrap Mr. Murray had asked them to save.

But through these many days, it was Lit Club that provided the real high points. The group continued to meet at the bookstore on Thursdays, and Worser continued to nab the seat next to Donya. Lee had introduced an entire village of characters in his elven kingdom but still hadn't begun the actual story, Felicity had presented two more haiku (one about a mockingbird and one about a dandelion), and Donya had shared a short story about an evil child who gets whatever he wants (clearly Seth in disguise). But Mae still only talked about her writing instead of showing any, Herbie didn't do either, and there were never submissions in the envelope at school, which shortened the meetings considerably. So Worser taught them more word games, and the group kept helping him with his Masterwork, suggesting words for his various entries or even new categories. Lee went so far as to sketch a series of whimsical animal mash-ups. Worser wasn't sure which one he liked best—the narwhallaby or the badgeraffe.

He had never known such a feeling of belonging. Somehow, he had attained a position of shared leadership with Donya, which made it extra rewarding. *Partners* was the word he liked best to describe it. They were truly *part* of each other's lives now.

On the first Thursday after this four-week stretch, a half hour before he had to leave for Lit Club, Worser was patrolling the perimeter of his dining room. As usual, he was eager to get to Re-Visions and could never sit still in the span of time between school and the meeting.

"Potato?" Aunt Iris appeared in the threshold to the kitchen, shouldering her large woven purse. "I need to run to the art supply store. Could you keep an eye on your mother? Perhaps go read to her?"

"But I need to be at my meeting by five!" He pointed to the cartoon boy on the gargantuan wall calendar, beside which he had written his departure for and return from the Lit Club meeting in thick Sharpie.

"I'll be back by then. The store is very close. Besides, it's just barely after four." She pointed to her watch as if he could read the face. "Just keep her company for a while. She and I worked on her buttoning skills today, and she did such a terrific job. You should be so proud of her."

"I am proud." Worser noted how defensive he sounded.

"It's inspiring, the progress she's made. She has that important checkup next month, you know."

"Of course, I know." Indeed, it was hard to miss the bright purple APPOINTMENT! on the next month's page, which was visible through this month's sheet. But also, his aunt had been talking about it for days. She seemed eager to hear the doctor's assessment. Perhaps she wanted proof of her caretaking magic—or a trophy.

"Go on, Potato. Seeing you is such a comfort to her, and it really motivates her to try harder at her therapies."

Worser again glanced at the calendar. Perhaps, at this next appointment, the doctor would give his forecast for when things would go back to normal. No more garish boxes in the living room. No more murderous beasts under the furniture. No more Aunt Iris taking over his life.

He'd write Aunt Iris's move-out date himself in all caps with the brightest marker.

"Fine, I'll sit with her," he said. "Just don't make me late."

"Felicity is a little too creative with language. She says *bitey things* when she means *mosquitoes* and emphasizes the wrong syllable in certain words—like *UH-mazing, UH-dorable, DEE-licious.* Sometimes she even adds an unnecessary syllable, like *okay-ee.*"

Worser hadn't found anything he wanted to read to his mother as he sat with her, so he launched into some idle talk instead. But a casual mention about what he planned to do the rest of the evening somehow turned into a detailed monologue on Lit Club and its members.

He went on to explain how Felicity resembled a twee storybook character, and how he imagined she lived in a tidy cottage with an actual picket fence, window boxes spilling over with flowers, and a whole menagerie of dainty pets—bunnies, ducklings, a coltish colt, and a doe-eyed doe.

"She's fanatical about animals for some reason, and she writes nature haiku. Last week she told us she wanted to start signing her name with an *F* followed by a heart shape—until I pointed out that some might interpret that as a pictogram for *fart.*"

He paused to check for a reaction.

His mother blinked at him. It was still difficult to look at her—largely because of the ridiculous headband his aunt had recently given her (pink with cat ears), but also because that searching stare of hers still made him feel self-conscious. And yet, sometimes when he met her gaze, he'd see a trace of the mother he'd always known. A flicker in her eye, a wiggle of her eyebrow, or a sputter of breath. It would only be there a few seconds, just long enough to remind him, before disappearing.

"Then there's Lee," Worser went on. "He's working on an epic fantasy, but so far, it's all world-building. I think he's only writing a novel so that he can illustrate it—and his drawings are quite good. When he reads his story aloud, he does it in a sort of British accent—which is odd because he said his family is from Mexico.

"Mae is interesting. She's supposedly writing some gothic thriller, but I've yet to hear any of it. She probably hasn't even started. But she's good at giving Lee criticism, so she at least knows what doesn't work in writing. She also appreciates puns. The other day I asked her, 'May I borrow a pen?' She handed me one and said, 'You may,' and I said, 'No, *you* Mae,' and she laughed.

"I'm not exactly sure why Herbie goes. He does enjoy books—sci-fi, especially—but I doubt he's even thought about writing anything. I guess he just enjoys the group. He's pretty much up for anything, really.

"That's all of them, except for Donya and me." Worser paused to savor the phrase *Donya and me*. "You're already quite familiar with the two of us."

He blinked and glanced around the room, remembering where he was.

"Anyway..." All at once he felt nervous. "Not much else to say except...I like it. These people. They like words. Like we do."

He wondered if he would find disappointment in his mother's expression for his simplistic vocabulary and syntax—or scorn over his associating with triflers and abecedarians. Maybe even pain that he brought up the club members' shared love of words when she was still struggling to utter basic sounds.

Instead, there was a softness in her eyes he couldn't recall seeing before. It looked like kindness or maybe relief.

It looked like love.

During the last few club gatherings, Worser had gotten into the habit of purchasing and donating his books to Re-Visions before the group arrived—so that he could spend more time with Donya afterward and be ready to take her up on the offer of a ride, should she ask again.

Today, as he stood at the sales counter, he had the distinct feeling that something was amiss.

Worser squinted at Mr. Murray. "You've changed something," he said.

"What are you talking about?"

"Oh, now I see. You've shaved." Gone was the ever-present crop of whiskers on Mr. Murray's chin. His face looked so naked, so revealing, Worser almost couldn't bear to look at it. So he didn't. That's when he noticed the suit. "You're also wearing different clothes. Why are you dressed up?"

"I had a meeting—not that it's any of your concern."

"What kind of a meeting?"

"A business meeting. What's it to you?" Mr. Murray glanced around the store. "Where's your friend? The funny-looking kid? He's usually the one with the questions."

"He's not coming. He outgrew his new shoes in less than

two months, so his Nanna is taking them out to the mall to try to exchange them."

"That kid's still growing? Yeesh."

Just then, the bells over the door rang out and Donya entered the store. She wore the barest of smiles, and her movements had a languid quality about them, as if she were performing an underwater ballet.

"Hey, Worser," she said as she passed. "Hello, Mr. Murray."

Mr. Murray grunted. Worser said hi, but it came out more as air than voice.

He again had the disquieting sense that things weren't right—not wrong exactly, but modified to an uncomfortable degree. Like a photo that's slightly out of focus or a song that's not quite in tune.

He left his purchases on the counter and followed Donya to the worktable, claiming the chair on her right, as usual. From there, he studied her closely as she unpacked items from her backpack.

"Um, can I help you?" She turned to face him. "Why are you staring at me?'

That's when he saw. "Why are you wearing eye makeup?"

"Why do you care?"

"It's just strange that your appearance and Mr. Murray's are both altered today."

Donya didn't reply.

"I thought it was an interesting coincidence."

She fiddled mindlessly with a stack of folders.

"That's all."

Her silence worried him. He wanted to say something that would bring her smile back—or at least engage her in conversation.

"Except to say...I think your eyes look better without all those products covering them," he added. "And Mom always said they cause cancer in lab animals."

Donya made a huffing sound and rose from her seat. She didn't return until the others arrived and it was time to start the meeting.

"People—I have news," Donya announced.

Worser was glad to see that her grin had returned. She stood holding an orange file upright, tapping the bottom edge against the tabletop.

"Todayyy," she began, drawing out the word, "we have an anonymous submission."

The Lit Club gave a collective gasp.

"Wait...what?"

"For real?"

"We actually got something in the envelope? And it isn't garbage?"

Donya nodded, her smile widening. "I brought copies for everyone." She handed around photocopies of a page full of angular handwriting. At the top was a title in all caps: LONESOME LOVE.

Worser glanced it over. "These appear to be song lyrics."

Donya settled into her seat beside him. "What makes you say so?"

"The repetition of lines. Also *ooh* isn't used much in poetry."

"So what if they are?" Donya asked with a shrug. "We have no rule against song lyrics. It's writing. There's absolutely nothing wrong with it."

"Except that they aren't good lyrics," Worser added.

Donya's mouth bunched up like the top of a drawstring bag. "Why would you say that?"

"Because I'm reading them. They're half-witted at best, nonsensical at worst. Like this line: *Take the man from woman. You get wo.* What does that even mean?"

"It sounds to me like it's supposed to be *woe*, as in *w-o-e*," Felicity commented.

"It sounds to me vaguely heteronormative," Mae said. "But also, maybe it's *whoa*, as in *w-h-o-a*. You wouldn't be able to tell the two apart when singing it."

"Which is why it should make sense in writing," Worser said. "And three lines down from that, what is this word: *a-m-i-r-i-t-e*?"

"It's short for *am I right*," Mae said.

"Ohhh," Lee said. "I thought it was a semiprecious stone."

"It may not be a candy wrapper, but it's still trash," Worser said. "Clearly he needs to do several editing passes or, better yet, choose another pursuit."

Donya's cheeks quivered, as if she were clenching and unclenching her jaw. "How do you even know the writer's a he?"

"I don't. But I'm assuming that's the case, since there are a number of places where he discusses being a man." Worser pointed to one of the offending lines. "Which, by the way, he rhymes with *different than*. It should be *different from*."

As he talked, Donya fixed him with a stare. There was something familiar about the way her features angled and narrowed. It wasn't until later that he recognized it: hers was the same expression Seer would wear before raking him with his claws.

In the moment, Worser could only sense that Donya's

mood had changed from good to bad, but he had no idea why. Could *she* be Anonymous? Surely not. The mere thought that the girl he'd been worshipping for eight years could author such tripe made his heart shrivel. Besides, it wasn't her handwriting anyway. No, something else was upsetting her. Perhaps her family. Or a teacher. Sometimes even the most minor of infractions could rouse Donya's temper.

Donya smiled again. But it was without the usual lift and sparkle in her eyes, so it came off as if she were baring her teeth. "Fine. That's all the feedback on this for now."

"But are we saying it's fit to print? How are we supposed to give the feedback to Anonymous if he's anonymous?" Felicity asked.

"Doesn't matter," Donya said, snatching the copies out of people's hands and shoving them back into the file. "We should move on. Who's next?"

Nobody spoke.

Donya turned toward Lee. "What about you? Any new writing or drawings?"

Lee shook his head. "I'm not ready to share again yet."

"Mae?"

"Still not done."

"Felicity?"

Felicity shook her head. "What about you, Donya? Do you have anything new?"

Donya sagged somewhat guiltily. "I've been busy. I'm doing lots of tutoring." She glanced from face to face. "Anyone? Don't tell me the meeting is over already."

"Actually," Felicity said, wrinkling her nose, "I was hoping we could help Worser with his lexicon again."

"Me too," Mae said. "I sorta had an entry idea."

A chorus of "What is it?" rose up from the table. Donya, Worser noted, pushed her chair back and crossed her arms, hugging the orange file to her chest.

Mae's suggestion was a list she called Smash the Patriarchy! "I was thinking we could revamp words where the syllable *man* would be replaced by *person*," she explained. "Like *personuscript* instead of *manuscript*."

"*Personual* instead of *manual*," Lee offered.

"*Personatee* instead of *manatee!*" added Felicity.

"Most of the time, the syllable *man* stems from the Latin root meaning 'hand' and not the male gender," Worser pointed out. He couldn't bring himself to tell the club that this topic was too nonsensical to be added to his Masterwork. "But," he added quickly, noting the disappointment on their faces, "it has merit as an exercise and...could be fun."

"All right," Mae said, pulling out a sheet of paper. "Let's do this."

"Oh goody," Donya muttered.

"All right. There's my dad. Need a ride or anything?" Mae asked.

"No. I have something I need to tend to." Worser hoped his answer was clear enough to end the discussion, but vague enough to not be a lie. The only thing he had to tend to was Donya.

"Okay, cool. See ya."

Mae left, and the familiar calm settled over him. The store fell silent, the only sound the turning of pages as Mr. Murray sat reading behind the sales counter. Donya stood at the front window with her forehead pressed against the glass. Worser went to stand beside her.

"You've really fired up the group with that lexicon of yours," she mumbled. Her breath made an oval-shaped patch of fog on the glass.

"Yes. Things are going quite well."

Donya snorted. "No, they aren't."

"They...aren't?"

"Things, if you haven't noticed—and I'm sure you haven't—are total crap."

Crap? Worser frowned. The word was vulgar. Overused. But also, this wasn't at all what was supposed to happen. Donya was supposed to thank him for rescuing the meeting from boredom after its members arrived unprepared. She was supposed to compliment him, engage in clever banter, perhaps even continue the banter during a shared ride home—if she ever offered him a ride again.

"What do you mean?" he asked.

"What do you mean, what do I mean? Everything's wrong!" Donya threw up her hands. "We're supposed to be reading and discussing our writing and gathering submissions for a magazine, not playing word games. Besides, this was supposed to be *my* break from the world, *my* solace. Now it's just you and your lexicon. And your smug criticism of other people's hard work."

Worser swallowed. "Those lyrics—that was your submission?"

"No." Donya's pitch lowered and her gaze dropped to the floor. "It belongs to a friend of mine. Someone I hoped might join the group. But now...I don't know. I'm not sure *I* even want to come anymore."

Worser was suddenly drowning in panic. "I...I'm sorry. I thought the feedback would be helpful. But it's also true that

I was showing off my superior use of language. It's...how I was raised."

Donya's mouth curled into a half smile. "Yeah, your mom was a hard-ass. I've heard the stories."

"This is your club. I'll step aside. No more group help on my Masterwork." His voice was raspy, and his hands were cold and trembling. "And tell your friend to come. Please? Please? Please?" Suddenly Worser couldn't stop saying please. It was his only word. His only thought.

Donya let out a sigh. "If I do stay, and if my friend does come, will you be kind with your criticism?"

Worser opened his mouth to reply.

"Let me rephrase," she interrupted. "Could you maybe not criticize at all for a while—just until the friend feels more at home in the group?"

Her request seemed to go against the very purpose of the club, but Worser felt he shouldn't point this out. "Of course."

"All right, then." She held out her hand. "Deal."

Headlights swept past as they shook on it.

"Here's my dad." With that, she pushed through the door and disappeared into the gathering darkness beyond.

"Hey, kid? Kid!"

Worser was still standing in the same spot by the window. His happy feeling had been blown to fragments—one piece sad, another worried, another bewildered. He had somehow displeased Donya by doing the very thing that had pleased her before. Luckily, they had reached an understanding before she left, but he was still reeling from the conversation and her possible departure from the club.

The patch of fog her breath had made on the glass was

still there, disappearing gradually. He watched as it dwindled to the size of a cherry, then a pea, then...nothing.

"Kid!"

Mr. Murray's voice made him jump. Worser turned to face him.

The store owner was waving him over. "Come here. I need to talk with you for a sec."

Worser scanned the window one last time for any trace of Donya—sadly, there was none—and trudged over. "I'm sorry about all that," he said.

"What?"

"The argument just now. I assume that's what you want to speak with me about."

"Eh, you kids. It's all the same crazy commotion to me."

"Do you need me to buy more books?"

"No, no. Listen." The man blew out his breath.

Worser was again struck by how different he looked today. With his face shaved and his hair slicked down, he appeared somehow smaller.

"I hate to say this, but...your club might have to start meeting somewhere else."

"Because of the commotion?"

"No. I mean, sure, you guys make it so I have to pop a few Advil on meeting nights, but that's not the problem. You see, my lease is up, and the jerk landlord is raising rent. And the plain truth is, I can't pay it."

Worser's fragments shattered into even more fragments.

"Are you certain?"

"Of course I am. I talked to my bookkeeper and other eggheads today. They've crunched numbers and done whatever else it is that they do. There's no way out."

"What will you do?"

"I'll have to close the store. I'm sorry, kid."

"No. No." Just as *Please* had been his refrain with Donya, now *No* was the word that reverberated through him. "When would you have to close?"

"I have till the end of December."

Worser paced about—he couldn't help it, even though he knew Mr. Murray detested it. As the diverse emotional shards clattered about inside him, he tried to come up with the right, logical response.

Eventually, he settled on begging.

"Please don't tell anyone else, okay? I'm sure there's a solution, and I'll help find it! Just...please don't tell Donya or the rest of the group." He paused to steady his breath. "Do I have your word?"

If *No* was Worser's word, what was Mr. Murray's?

"Whatever, kid."

There was something different about his house, too.

At first, Worser couldn't put his finger on it, but from half a block away, he could sense it. He took note of the structure as he approached. Paint? As far as he could tell in the twilight, it was the same as always—a faded neutral beige, like a papyrus scroll. Cars? His mom's brown Altima and his aunt's orange Volkswagen were parked out front, as usual. Yard? Still the same neglected tufts of grass and clover. Same rocks, like broken teeth, edging the lawn.

He got his answer when he headed down the driveway. The porch—it was in clear view. Which meant the curtain of dead or dying spider plants had been taken down. His aunt must have done it while he was at Lit Club.

It surprised Worser how sad he felt about it. He hadn't exactly loved the plants—as evidenced by their slow demise—nor did he spend a great deal of time on the porch. Still, he felt violated. The rattling sensation that had begun at the store was now shaping itself into anger.

Worser thumped through the front door and immediately stopped short. Drops of red stood out on the foyer's gold vinyl floor tiles. His heart started a new, faster rhythm.

Slowly, tentatively, he followed the drops around the corner. In the dining room, he saw green drops along with the red. Then purple. "What?" he said aloud.

"Potato? Is that you?"

"Be?"

The voices came from the living room. No one sounded upset or in distress.

Entering the room, he found his aunt and mother sitting on stools in front of an easel, with a stained drop cloth underneath them. Both were wearing peculiar garments. Looking closer, Worser recognized them as their once-blue, now-gray bath towels with holes cut in the middle so that they could be worn as smocks.

"Hello!" Aunt Iris waved a multicolored hand at him. "There's some split pea soup for you on the stove. Have some and then come join us! Your mother had an extra-long nap today and isn't sleepy yet, so we're having some fun. Aren't we, Constance?"

Worser gestured about the room. "What is this nonsense?"

"Why do you sound so vexed?" Aunt Iris asked. "Haven't you ever finger-painted?"

"Not since kindergarten."

"I bet you enjoyed it then."

"I'm quite sure I didn't. You've ruined our towels. How irresponsible."

"These?" Aunt Iris grabbed a corner of her makeshift smock. "They're as thin as paper. Completely useless. So we picked out new ones this afternoon, didn't we, Constance? Bright purple ones."

His mother grinned.

Worser dropped his backpack with a satisfying thud. "Mom shouldn't be doing this so late. You'll ruin her health."

Aunt Iris laughed, which enraged him even more. "Oh, don't be silly. We're just finishing up. Plus, this is good therapy for her." She made a waving motion that splattered paint all over herself. "Come look at what she's made."

In spite of his outrage, Worser was curious—and also hoped to find more evidence of his aunt's wrongdoing. He circled around to stand between them, facing the easel.

"Isn't it lovely?"

He studied the image but saw only multicolored streaks flying every which way—as if someone had detonated a rainbow. "What is it?"

"It isn't anything. It's a beautiful mix of colors. Finger painting is best when you aren't trying to re-create actual things, don't you agree?"

Worser didn't agree. But he did have a vague sense that perhaps all those years ago, when he'd attempted finger painting in preschool and disliked it, it was because he'd done it wrong. He'd actually tried to paint something in particular. In fact, he'd painted fingers—although it hadn't come out looking like a hand the way he'd intended. More like a sloppy, multicolored asterisk.

"Besides, the finger strokes are good for her fine motor

skills. Watch." Aunt Iris gently lifted his mother's right wrist and guided it to the canvas. "And stroke! And stroke!"

Worser put his hands over his ears and took three lurching steps backward.

"Very good, Constance. And stroke! And stroke!"

Each exclamation from his aunt was like a tremor, shaking him to the core. "SHUT UP!" He felt the words explode out of him.

The two women turned and gaped. His mother, he noticed, had a spot of green near the tip of her nose.

"Potato?" Aunt Iris said. "What's wrong? You've gone pale."

"I just... Stop saying that word. *Please!*"

"What word?" she asked.

He saw the realization gradually come over his aunt.

"Oh my," she said. "I'm sorry. I didn't know what I was saying. I'm so sorry."

The view before him changed suddenly. Worser was no longer in the living room, but back outside. He found that he was running. It wasn't until he saw the shape of the tree line that he realized where his feet were taking him.

The world outside was so dusky and quiet that it seemed to be on pause. Luckily, the electric glow of the town illuminated the sky well enough to help him find his way. He could hear the iambic tempo of his footfall, the snap of every twig, and his ragged breaths as he climbed the rungs to his special hideaway and collapsed in a heap of exhaustion on the platform.

Once his vital signs began to slow to normal, he pushed himself upright, leaned back against the tree trunk and pulled his knees to his chest. He had no backpack, no Masterwork, and hardly any light—nothing to occupy his thoughts. All he could do was stare out into the gloom. But with very little to see around him, the images in the back of his mind zoomed into focus, taking on shape and color.

Worser. Five months earlier. Coming downstairs after an afternoon of writing.

He had made himself a snack first—that's what would haunt him most, later on—a piece of white bread smeared with blueberry jam. After fishing a cleanish-looking dish from the sink, he took his food into the living room.

"Mom?"

She'd been lying on the floor beside the couch—as if she'd rolled off or had tried to reach it and couldn't quite make it.

Everything that came after was a jumble. His frantic knock on Ms. Lucretia's door. Their call to Aunt Iris. The paramedics who'd rushed into the living room. (Had they let themselves into the house? Or did he go to the door? He couldn't recall.) Through some combination of actions, he'd ended up at the hospital and, at some point, his aunt joined him in the waiting room. It was all fuzzy and dreamlike, those images—nothing like the stark picture of his mother lying motionless on the rug, mouth in a lopsided grimace, the stench of urine hanging in the air.

He had thought she was dead. And in those moments, he'd felt utterly alone. Cold. Helpless. A kite unleashed in a storm.

The feeling had never quite gone away.

THIRTEEN

Offense

The next Tuesday, Worser found himself in a somewhat familiar spot. Principal Ludlum was slumped over his desk, elbows propped, head resting in his hands. This gave Worser, who was once again sitting across from him, a perfect view of his bald spot. There was a cluster of small moles on the bare patch of skin that reminded him of the Little Dipper, and Worser had a sudden and bizarre urge to connect the dots. But he didn't have his Sharpie anymore, and even if he had, the gratification it would provide would have been too fleeting and not worth the resulting fuss.

"Will, what are we going to do with you?" Mr. Ludlum asked as he lifted his head.

"Who?"

"You."

"You misunderstand." Worser shook his head. "I meant, who are the *we* in your question?"

"I mean the school."

"The building?"

Mr. Ludlum closed his eyes in a wincing sort of way. "The people who run this school."

"Oh. You mean you."

"My point is, this is the third time we've met here since school began. That's worrisome. Tell me, Will, what is it that you think you're doing?"

"At present I'm sitting in this chair, answering your questions."

"I suppose you think that's clever. You know very well I'm asking why you were brought before me today."

"Coach Tolliver sent me here."

"That part I know. But why?"

"I was correcting a glaring grammatical error, and, for some reason, this upset her. She also took away my Sharpie."

Mr. Ludlum lifted the referral form. "Defacing school property," he read, each word lower on the scale, creating a sad-trombone effect.

"The poster in the hall said 'Titans *extract* revenge' instead of *exact* revenge," Worser explained. "In ten-inch-high block letters in primary colors. It was a linguistic travesty—not to mention an eyesore."

"She also says you wouldn't stop arguing and that you used a rude phrase."

"That is false. It was Coach Tolliver who used a vulgar and imprecise expression. I simply pointed it out to her."

Principal Ludlum slumped again.

Smelling victory, Worser pled his case: When he'd tried to explain to Coach Tolliver that he was using the red Sharpie to correct an egregious error, pulling out his pocket dictionary for reference, she told him to "nip it in the butt." Worser then pointed out that *butt* should be *bud*, and that the phrase came from gardeners who pinch off young buds to stop plants from flowering too soon or too much. Telling him to nip it in the *butt* made no sense, he explained, in that it implied he should bite something in the rear end. That's when Coach Tolliver got out the referral form.

"One would think," Worser concluded, "that an institution dedicated to teaching young minds would commend someone who takes it upon himself to correct inaccurate wording."

It offended him that his efforts to improve language use had never been appreciated. This latest ordeal reminded him of the previous spring when Porter Cosgrove wrote a Valentine's Dance "proposal" to Mindy Herrington on their social studies teacher's blackboard. Worser had explained that in the sentence "I await your reply with baited breath," *baited* should be spelled *bated*—which meant a slowing of one's breathing. "*Baited* with an *i*," he had said, "suggests that your breath is evocative of worms and fish hooks." The other students had laughed at that, and Porter felt the need to dump nightcrawlers on his head the next day.

"The bottom line is, we cannot keep having these infractions." Surprisingly, Mr. Ludlum was sitting straight and looking him in the eye. "You are not one of the faculty. Rules exist for a reason, and they are for all students."

Worser stared down at his hands. He had to admit to himself that this instance had been different. It wasn't just the horrid malapropism that had prompted him to write on the poster. This time, unlike with his previous referrals, he'd realized he was doing something wrong in the eyes of authority—but he chose not to heed that knowledge. He was simply fed up with things being wrong, and all the frustration, fear, and new nameless emotions roiling inside him had seized the opportunity to lash out.

The truth was, it had felt good to deface the sign. He'd even experienced a sort of quiet glee when the coach confronted him. Only now the satisfaction was spent.

"Fine," he said. "I'm willing to reimburse for the cost of the poster board."

Remarkably, the offer was turned down. Principal Ludlum believed that Worser had been given enough chances and that it was time to take stronger measures. Papers were filled out and a directive was given.

"You will report to lunch detention in room 212."

"This is absurd," Worser said as the documents were handed to him. "An absolute miscarriage of justice."

"These are the consequences for flaunting the rules, young man."

"I'm *flouting* the rules," Worser corrected. "And you're flaunting your power."

Principal Ludlum ignored the jibe. "Detention was earned by you, not given by me," he said. "I really hope that you will use the time to think about what's important to you."

"Herbie!" Worser kept an eye on the familiar curly hair a few yards ahead of him in the corridor. "Herbie!"

His friend continued loping toward the cafeteria, oblivious to Worser's shouts.

Worser darted around and between excruciatingly slow students. He was especially irritated by the ones who walked in a row of four or more down the hallway, like a human wall—an apathetic Greek phalanx with smartphones.

In the back of his mind, he wondered why he seemed to be running all the time lately. He never used to. In fact, he'd avoided it as a rule—going so far as to walk the 50-yard dash in PE two years before, a feat that had prompted his teacher to make an ill-advised phone call to his mother. Lately, though, life was happening at a different speed. Lately, there were so many things to rush toward. Or from.

"Herbie!"

At last, Herbie heard his calls. "Hey," he said in greeting as Worser closed the gap between them. "I thought you were absent. You weren't in the nook this morning."

"I was…" Worser paused to catch his breath. "I was hauled into the office on a referral."

Herbie's eyebrows flew toward his scalp.

"I only have a minute," Worser went on, still short of breath. "I have to report to lunch detention. But I need to give you some bad news: Mr. Murray's rent is going up and he's going to have to close Re-Visions."

This time, Herbie's mouth fell open in surprise.

"And I wanted to see if you could come over after school today, so we could figure out how to stop that from happening."

At this point, Herbie's entire head jutted forward, as if the brainpower needed to process this astonishing news was too much for his poor skull. "You want me to come over?" he finally said.

"Is that all right?" Worser asked, suddenly worried. It hadn't occurred to him that Herbie might say no.

Herbie shrugged. "Probably. I'll call Nanna from the office and let her know. But what happened with—"

"No time," Worser said, cutting him off. "I'll apprise you of the situation after geography."

With that, Worser turned and restarted his run.

❖❖❖

Worser made it to room 212 with three minutes to spare. He collapsed into a seat in a relatively unpopulated section of the room and tried to catch his breath.

"Library Boy!"

The voice was familiar, and it evoked a vague feeling of unease. Turning toward the sound, Worser saw Turk striding down the row of desks, looking right at him. For some reason, he was wearing a knit cap on his head, even though it was 80 degrees Fahrenheit outside.

Turk sank into the seat in front of him and immediately spun about to face him. "Whoa that you're here."

Worser wondered if it was possible that Mr. Ludlum knew Turk's presence would add to his punishment.

"Turk Thibodeaux, this is detention," the teacher at the front of the room called out—rather obviously Worser thought. "No talking."

Turk grinned back at her. "It's not detention yet. Clockwise, it's in two minutes. I just want to say hi to my friend."

Worser was so stupefied at Turk referring to him as a friend that he overlooked his misuse of *clockwise*. He also dropped his pen, which rolled beneath his desk. There followed an embarrassing scramble to retrieve it, which caused him to bang his head. When he sat back up, Turk had slung his arm around the top of his chair to cushion his chin while he stared at Worser.

"I thought you were a good student. Straight A-plus," Turk said. "What brings you here?"

"Defacing school property."

"High fiveage!"

Turk lifted his hand, and, Worser, seemingly on autopilot, clapped him back.

"I also supposedly mouthed off to Coach Tolliver," Worser added.

"No way. You? Why so rudimentary?"

Worser cringed. Obviously, this was part of his penance for the illegal grammar fix—to sit behind someone who regularly butchered language. Prosaic justice.

Turk was still waiting for a reply.

"I..." Worser paused, wondering how to explain it. "I have problems with authority."

The man-boy grinned and lifted his hand again, and again Worser slapped it without thinking.

"Why are you here?" Worser asked.

"Not sure," Turk pondered. "Could be the tardies. Or skipping seventh period. No wait." He raised his finger. "I was caught making out with my girlfriend next to the soda machine. She got off with a warning."

"All right. Time's up," the teacher called out. "Turk, everyone, eat your lunch and no talking."

"Excuse me?" Worser waved his hand in the air. "What if you don't have a lunch?"

"Detention students are supposed to grab a sack lunch in the cafeteria before the bell if they didn't bring one from home. It is clearly stated on your copy of the detention form. If you did not do so, I can allow you to go get one. But understand that this will make you tardy and add on another day of lunch detention."

Worser considered debating the matter but decided against it. He had been so indignant at being given the punishment, and then so intent on catching Herbie, that he hadn't read anything on the form beyond the room number. Thankfully, he remembered he still had a granola bar his aunt had slipped into his bag weeks before.

"No need," he said. "I have something to eat."

"Fine. Now, *no talking*."

He found the battered, broken bar at the bottom of his backpack, ate it, and tossed the wrapper. Then he got out his homework.

"No homework," the teacher called to him.

"That's outrageous."

"No talking!" the teacher said. "This is detention, not study hall. You are to sit quietly and think about your transgression."

Worser gathered up his papers and shoved them back into his pack. He then sat quietly—but as disobediently as possible. Mr. Ludlum had told him to think about what was important to him, but he wouldn't give him the satisfaction.

Of course, in his efforts *not* to think about what he found important, he ended up doing so anyway. Numerous things that mattered to him defiantly conjured themselves in his mind. Lit Club. Writing his Masterwork. The bookstore. Donya. Donya. Donya. His thoughts were a vibrant mess, just like his mother's painting. So many of those things were in danger of going away.

As he sat and tried not to think, and thought anyway, Worser was reminded of the science museum on the campus where his mother worked—a place he'd visited a few times over the years. It was full of exhibits, specimens, and detailed accounts of things that had come to a standstill. Prehistoric insects suspended in amber. Woolly mammoths frozen in glaciers. Ancient humans swallowed and preserved by bogs.

He wanted to postpone the rest of his life in such a way. Not to perish, but to contain his existence and put it in an enormous pickling jar—so that everything could stay the same.

Everything, that is, except his mother. She needed to continue progressing so that their life together could go back to the way it used to be.

After school, Herbie walked with Worser to his house. It was an exhausting trek. Not because they hurried—in fact, Herbie loped along at his usual pace. But Worser had to take three steps for every one of Herbie's, until he finally grew tired and resorted to calling out directions from behind.

Eventually, he shouted for Herbie to stop.

Herbie stood at the edge of the lawn, waiting. "Is this your house? I like it. It looks like a boot," he said once Worser had caught up to him.

Worser tilted his head to the same angle as Herbie's. Sure enough, he saw it—the porch was the toe area and the two-story house was the main part of the boot.

Even though he was eager to get started, Worser first led Herbie into the kitchen. Having not had much lunch, he decided to grab some food to help fuel their brainstorming. They had just loaded up a plate with scone-stones when Aunt Iris appeared carrying a laundry basket.

"Potato? Is that you?" she said. She caught sight of Herbie and gave a start. "Oh! Excuse me. I didn't realize anyone else was here."

"This is Herbie."

"Hi." Herbie bobbed his head in greeting.

Aunt Iris glanced from Herbie to Worser and back again.

Her expression was similar to Herbie's elongated look of surprise at lunchtime—eyebrows up, lower jaw down. "Why, hello," she said, eventually. "Welcome."

"This is my aunt," Worser explained, lest Herbie assume she was his mother. "She's...staying here awhile."

"Please call me Iris."

"Why do you call him Potato?" Herbie asked.

"Oh, that." Aunt Iris laughed. "When he was a baby, he had the cutest bald head—all oval-shaped and soft with the barest bit of fuzz. I started calling him Potato Head and then shortened it to Potato. I guess it just stuck!"

"Nanna calls me Pumpkin, but I don't think it's because of my head." Herbie looked thoughtful. "Maybe. I should ask her."

"Well, I have to go finish up the laundry," Aunt Iris said. "When you're done here, Potato, please go say hello to your mother. She's sitting in her p-ohm."

Worser was aghast. "You put her in one of those contraptions? In her condition?"

"No, no. I realized my p-ohms weren't all-accessible, so I'm experimenting with a different model, and I made one just for her. She's my beta tester." Aunt Iris looked very pleased with herself.

"You boys have fun." Aunt Iris balanced the laundry basket against her hip as she reached for the door of the garage-utility room with her other hand. "Very nice to meet you, Herbie."

"You too." Herbie gave a vigorous wave, as if she were leaving on a cruise ship. "I like her," he said, after the door closed behind her. "She smells like church."

Herbie seemed only mildly surprised that the main living

area of Worser's house was filled with brightly painted crates. Thankfully, there was more room to move about after the recent sale of Peace and Wisdom.

In the middle of the space stood a new, tent-like object made of dark blue cloth. Worser peered inside and saw his mother, sitting in a rattan chair. On the fabric wall opposite her was the word *Believe* in hand-lettered gold script.

"Hi, Mom," Worser said in a whisper. "I'm home."

She pivoted toward him. "Be," she said, her eyes bright.

"This is Herbie." Worser lifted the flap wider to reveal his friend.

"Be," she said again.

"We'll be in my room. Um...carry on." He closed the flap and tiptoed away. Herbie followed, also treading softly. Worser wasn't sure why he was whispering and tiptoeing, only that it felt appropriate.

"Is your mom all right?" Herbie asked once they'd reached the foyer.

"She...had an accident," Worser replied. It wasn't the truth—not really—and he felt a twinge of guilt. He realized he was being irrational, but he still refused to utter the word *stroke*, afraid it might give it more power. "But she's getting better," he added.

Herbie nodded. "My mom drinks too much booze," he said. His voice was matter-of-fact, but his eyes drooped at an angle Worser had never seen before. "Nanna says she will come back when she stops for good. In the meantime, we all pray for her—me, Nanna, and our whole congregation. We'll pray for your mom, too."

"Thanks," Worser said.

As they entered Worser's bedroom, Herbie sniffed the air.

"Your room kind of smells like when our cheese goes bad." He turned in a slow circle. "How come you don't have any posters up?"

"They're distasteful." Worser knew teenagers were supposed to paper their walls with pictures of pouty young adults who never seemed to button their clothes all the way up, but he never understood why. "Do you have posters on your walls?"

"I have a Star Trek poster and a calendar of the world's most delicious tacos," Herbie said, sitting cross-legged on the carpet. "Aww. I didn't know you had a cat." He reached forward, as Seer was emerging from beneath the bed.

"Be careful. He's a rancorous and bloodthirsty beast."

To Worser's utter amazement, Seer padded right up to Herbie and began rubbing against him.

"He's sweet. What's his name?"

"Seer."

"Seer?"

"It's short for Seersucker. He has a sister, a calico named Ging—short for Gingham. My aunt found them in the parking lot of a fabric store."

"Your aunt is a good person."

Worser opened his mouth, ready to argue that what looked like kindness was actually a need to dominate—but he wasn't sure Herbie would understand, and time was limited.

He sat on his bed and balanced a pad of paper on his lap. "Now then, let's concentrate. We need viable suggestions on how we can help Mr. Murray."

"Tell me again," Herbie said with a mouthful of scone, "why is it up to us to help him?"

"Because..." Worser found himself at a loss for words—a

rare experience for him. Up to this point, he had been operating on pure emotion and instinct. He simply *had* to save the store. But now Herbie's question caused him to consider, in words, why it was so important to do so.

He found there were many reasons. If he lost the bookstore, he'd only have the tree house as a real sanctuary—and it wasn't as comfortable as Re-Visions and was useless in bad weather. Also, Lit Club would have no place to meet, which could spell the end of the club itself. Which would mean no more wordplay with others. No more being appreciated for his knowledge of words. And no more regularly scheduled hours with Donya.

Herbie was leaning toward him, expectantly. Worser had the words now, but he wasn't sure how to say them aloud—or if he wanted to.

"Because...," Worser repeated. He reached for an answer that didn't involve his lifelong love of Donya or his shattered emotional bits. "Our community doesn't have any other bookstores that aren't on campus. And access to books is a cornerstone of democracy."

"Oh. So if people aren't shopping at the bookstore, does that mean they don't want democracy?"

"They would be shopping there if they knew about the store. Bookstores have something for everyone. It's just a matter of publicizing."

"I don't know." Herbie reached for a second stone. "This seems to be an adult problem."

"Not entirely. If the bookstore closes, Lit Club won't have a place to meet."

"Oh yeah. Right." Herbie's face scrunched up in worry. "We should talk about it at the next meeting."

"No!" Worser shouted, whacking the pad of paper against his lap. He wasn't sure why he objected, only that he didn't want Donya to know he'd failed her. At present, she assumed that he and the bookstore were a package deal. If the group couldn't use the store, she might ask Worser to leave the club—especially with her being so upset about all the time they spent on his Masterwork. "No," he repeated. "Let's...not bother them with this."

"But what are we going to do?"

"That's what we're trying to figure out."

Herbie rested his chin in his hand and sighed. "I wish we were all rich and could just give Mr. Murray the money."

Worser had thought something similar. Ever since Mr. Murray had told him the bad news, he'd considered handing over all the money he had in the bank. But he knew it would only be a short-term solution. Plus, he probably couldn't empty his account without his mom's permission, and that, at present, was impossible. And even if she could help him access the funds, she probably wouldn't.

"We just need to bring more business to Re-Visions," Worser said. "Once he gets more customers on a regular basis, he'll be able to pay the higher rent. But how can we get the word out?"

"Hey, I know!" Herbie brightened up. "Let's put an ad in the paper!"

Worser shook his head. "That won't work."

The day before, he had called the local daily with the same idea. It was an institution he and his mom had long considered substandard and useless, but he was desperate. Unfortunately, the person on the other end kept tossing out terms like *composition* and *ratio* and *hi-res* until it was evident Worser was out of his depth.

"Surely there's another way," Worser said. "Can you recall an instance when advertising was effective? When you saw something and decided you had to try it?"

Herbie stared up at Worser's empty walls. "Well...there was one time when Nanna was driving down the road and this guy was juggling on a unicycle. We stopped to look and saw a sign next to him that read 'Big Top Snow Cones' with an arrow. The store was right behind him, so we went inside."

"Excellent!" Worser exclaimed.

"They were okay, but not excellent. I got brain freeze."

"No, I mean, that's what we need to do. That's how we'll advertise the store."

Herbie frowned. "But I don't have a unicycle, and I can only juggle one ball."

"It doesn't matter. All we have to do is stand in front of the store and attract attention."

"How are we going to do that?"

FOURTEEN

Patronize

"Are you sure this is going to work?" Herbie's voice sounded very far away, even though he stood right beside Worser.

"No, I'm not sure."

"Then why are we doing this?"

Worser looked down. It was unnerving hearing his friend's voice emanate from the head of a gorilla, and difficult to talk directly to it. "Because we have to try something. We can't just do nothing."

"It smells in this costume," Herbie remarked. "Like...hot dog burps."

"I'm sure you'll get used to it."

They were standing in the middle of the now nearly empty storage room, since the small bathroom didn't have enough room for the both of them and the giant gorilla suit.

"All right," Worser said, focusing on Herbie's brown eyes in the holes of the costume. "It's time to get started."

Together they left the storage room and headed out to the front, Worser leading the way since Herbie's vision was restricted. They found Mr. Murray in his usual spot—sitting on a tall stool behind the sales counter with his nose in a thick paperback.

"Eesh," he muttered when he saw Herbie. "Is this some kind of joke? One of those let's-scare-an-old-man kind of deals? Because it's going to take a lot more than that to give me a heart attack."

Herbie shook his giant primate head. "No. This is our great plan."

Mr. Murray frowned. "What'd he say?" he asked Worser.

"He said this is our plan to help you."

"How the hell is this supposed to help me?"

"By attracting attention," said the gorilla head.

"What?"

"He said it will attract attention."

"And that's good how?"

"People don't know about this store," Worser explained. "If they did, they would shop here. Then you'd earn more money and be able to pay the new lease amount."

"Whose big idea was this?"

"Mine."

"Then how come he's the one in the suit?"

"Well, originally we wanted an owl suit, to play into the 'wise old owl' stereotype—even though it's inaccurate, as owls aren't considered to have superior intelligence. The adage really should be 'wise old crow' or 'wise old parrot.'" Worser noticed the annoyed expression on Mr. Murray's face and got to the point. "Because of all the Halloween parties, the costume shop only had this one available. I didn't fit in it."

Mr. Murray gave one last grimace and returned to his book. "Whatever, kids. Just keep me out of it, okay?"

Worser led Herbie to the entrance and grabbed the homemade sign he'd stashed beside the door—a large poster-board arrow with **BOOKS!** lettered on it in black, bold caps.

"You know what you're supposed to do, right?" Worser asked.

The gorilla shrugged.

Worser sighed. "Stand out front in the parking lot and dance around with the sign."

"I'm not sure I can dance. The costume makes it hard to bend."

"Then gesture. Often. Use the sign to point people toward the store."

"Okay."

Worser pulled Herbie to the empty patch of the lot near Re-Visions. His prayers for good weather had been answered. It was sunny and very warm, even for Texas in October. Half the town appeared to be venturing out on this Saturday.

Once Herbie was properly positioned, Worser headed back into the store and observed through the front window. At first Herbie simply stood and gazed about. He then began moving his limbs, as if testing out how they worked. After a while, he tried out some movements. He pointed to Re-Visions. He lifted the arrow and shook it. He swung the sign in a grand sweeping motion toward the shop. He even tried to spin it a couple of times, but it always fell onto the asphalt after one or two rotations.

Gradually, people began to notice him. From his vantage point at the window, Worser could see pedestrians stop, stare, elbow people beside them, and laugh. A few even took pictures with their phones. Worser was near giddy. His plan was now fully in place.

Come inside, he urged in his mind. *Come in the store.* His knees were jiggling, and his hands were clasped tightly in front of him.

Sadly, the spectators would move on after their sighting, continuing toward other stores or their vehicles without even a glance toward the shop. Each time, Worser would feel a tightness in his throat, like a nascent whimper.

Come this way, he kept urging softly.

It continued like this for almost an hour. Gorilla Herbie would point and bounce as much as his furry armor allowed. People would pause and enjoy it. Worser would feel a prickling of hope. Yet no one entered the store.

Just as despair was setting in, Worser heard a high-pitched squeal. It was in the range of sounds that encompassed boiling tea kettles, sopranos, and electric drills. Not even Felicity could hit these notes.

"Eeeee! Monkey! Monkey! Monkey! Mama, look! Monkey!"

Eventually the source revealed itself. A small child was hopping down the walkway, yelling and pointing at Herbie. A woman appeared a few steps behind him, laden with bags and glancing at her phone.

"Umm-hmm," she replied absently.

"Yay monkey!"

The mother finally glanced up and noticed Herbie. "Oh yes. Look at that." Together, they stopped to watch the gorilla antics.

At this point they were right in front of the bookstore. *Come inside,* Worser implored silently. Miraculously, the woman turned and peered at the store, as if she'd heard him. Worser almost collapsed with relief when she grabbed her son by the hand and stepped through the door.

"Here, watch the monkey through the window. Mommy's going to look around a bit."

The woman acknowledged Worser with a smile, which he returned, so grateful that she'd followed his telepathic command.

"Yook," the boy said to Worser. "Monkey." He indicated Herbie by jabbing a pudgy index finger against the glass.

Worser wasn't sure how old the child was, having next to no experience with people younger than he. His mind tended to lump all individuals between babyhood and age five as those-who-can't-read-and-often-require-help-with-their-bathroom-needs.

"It isn't a monkey; it's a gorilla," Worser corrected. "Monkeys have tails."

The boy kept laughing and pressing his hands against the window. Streaks appeared on the glass. They glistened with wetness, and Worser did not want to know why.

"Ha! Ha, ha, ha!"

Every sound the child made seemed to be at an inhuman volume. It was unreasonable—and painful to endure at such close range. Worser could hear Mr. Murray *sheesh*ing behind him.

"Ha-ha! Silly monkey!"

Worser glanced back to see how the mother was faring. She was perusing a nearby bookcase, immune to the noise level and unaware of the store owner's distress. At the sales counter, Mr. Murray had his head propped in his hands, index fingers in his ears, forehead bunched up in agony. He noticed Worser staring and motioned him over.

"How long do I have to put up with this?" he muttered.

Worser shrugged. "I'm not sure how long his mother will take, but at least you have a customer."

"Boom! Hee! Ha-ha-ha!"

"I meant," Mr. Murray added, "how long are you and your pal going to keep up these shenanigans?"

"Fall down! Ha-ha-ha! Boom!"

"Oh. Well, we thought that..." Worser paused. It finally dawned on him what the child was shouting.

"Monkey fall down! Boom! Ha-ha!"

Worser and the mother hurried to the front window. Sure enough, Herbie lay supine on the concrete, his crumpled arrow lying beside him. A small crowd of onlookers had already begun gathering around.

"Oh my goodness!" the mother cried.

"Is monkey sleeping?"

Mr. Murray walked up beside Worser and let out a groaning sigh. "Kid. I know you're only trying to help, but this is the kind of attention I really don't need."

The good news was that Herbie did not have heat stroke. It was also good news that there was a man in the crowd, a nurse, who could step in and diagnose him.

Herbie was instructed to get out of the suit and into an air-conditioned building where he could lie down and sip water. Mr. Murray, Worser, and the nurse helped him into Re-Visions. He lay on the floor, propped by the discarded suit, sipping a Gulpee that Worser had fetched for him, and tripping unsuspecting customers—actually, one customer. Actually, one person who came in asking if Re-Visions was a costume shop and left as soon as he was told no. Still, Mr. Murray felt it was a hazard to have Herbie's long legs blocking the aisles.

"We already skirted disaster once today," he said. "Let's not keep asking for it."

They helped Herbie onto the large oak table, where he lay in repose until he felt like himself again. When Herbie noticed a stain on the ceiling that supposedly resembled a turtle in a party hat, Worser knew his cohort was back in form.

Worser had hoped that while Herbie lay semiconscious on the ground, the concerned onlookers would have at least noticed the sign. But, alas, the arrow had bent on impact, with only BOO being still visible—which lent credence to the myth, voiced by various onlookers, that the gorilla's antics had been a pre-Halloween celebration. At least a few bystanders had taken pictures of Herbie—which Worser could see as they held out their phones toward his sprawled form. His last shred of optimism was that they might mention the bookstore if they shared the images on social media.

"Sorry I passed out," Herbie said.

He looked so pitiful with his flushed face and wilted, sweaty curls that Worser wanted to lift his spirits. "Don't worry. At least the mom felt bad for us and bought a book. That's something." He remembered her making the purchase during all the commotion—then quickly leaving, holding the hand of her wailing toddler, who'd been upset that he couldn't play with the "sleeping monkey."

"That's good." Herbie looked somewhat cheered. "So what now?"

"Perhaps we could try again when it's cooler outside?" Worser suggested.

Herbie shook his head. "I don't think so. Being a gorilla is harder than it looks."

"I suppose you're right."

"Maybe we should tell the rest of Lit Club," Herbie said. "I bet they'd have ideas."

"No! I don't want to panic everyone if we can fix it on our own."

They brainstormed for the next half hour, until Worser felt as if he had been the one with near heat exhaustion. At one point, he glanced up and saw Mr. Murray leaning against the nearby bookcase, listening.

"Look, fellas. I can't have you interrupting what little business I have. Herbie seems fine now. Time to go home."

In light of the drama, the noise, and the stench emanating from the costume, Worser felt it was a fair request—they were done for the day.

So they packed up and took the city bus back to the costume shop, where Worser discovered he'd have to pay a $45 dry-cleaning bill on top of the rental fee—due to the fact that Herbie had fainted onto a puddle of melted mint chocolate chip.

"I did?" Herbie said. "Mmm. Now I want ice cream."

Worser shook his head. Advertising, it seemed, worked in mysterious ways.

FIFTEEN

Representation

When Worser got home, his mother was napping. He assumed Aunt Iris would be in the living room, working on her "art." To his surprise and annoyance, he found her standing in his room.

"Wouldn't you like to paint your walls?" she asked. Color strips were fanned out in her hand—blues, greens, yellows. It reminded him of his mother's finger painting.

"I would not."

"I just think it would be so much more cheerful if you did. And you could choose the shade you like best, so it would be an expression of who you are."

Worser squeezed his eyes shut. "Who I am is someone who prefers his walls colorless and unadorned. And his room free of visitors."

"Well, you need new carpet, you have to agree."

"I do not agree."

"It's probably why it smells in here. Besides, just listen to this." She shuffled the sole of her sandal. "Carpeting shouldn't crackle."

It was true that the cut pile had the dull, trampled

consistency of parched grass. But Worser had never in his life worried about the condition of his floor covering. It was carpet. It kept his feet warm and cushioned. It caught the crumbs of his snacks and absorbed any spills. As far as he was concerned, it was doing what it was supposed to do.

"Instead of you wasting money on new carpet," Worser said, "you should get my door fixed so that it will close and keep others out."

"Oh, I suppose we could do that," his aunt said, not picking up on the hint. "We should probably get you a new bed, too. Perhaps one with a trundle in case your friend Herbie wants to spend the night sometime."

"Why on earth would he want to sleep here when he presumably has a perfectly good bed of his own?"

"It's what friends do when they get together."

"Sleep?"

Aunt Iris let out one of her exaggerated sighs. "All I'm saying is that your room could be cleaner and more comfortable."

Worser clenched his jaw.

"We only want what's best for you, that's all," she said, pressing a blue color strip to the nearest wall.

There it was—what he objected to most. So much meaning in that one little word. Aunt Iris used *we*—as if she and his mother were of one mind.

"I like my room the way it is, and Mom does, too. *We* don't need your help!"

"Fine." Aunt Iris threw up her hands in a gesture of surrender. "I don't want to argue. I only want us to make the most of the day. Your mother and I would love to spend some time with you once she wakes up. Why don't you call up your little friend and we can all go to the movies?"

"My friend is not little, and I already saw him today. Besides, I don't enjoy movies. They usually aren't well written—a waste of words."

Aunt Iris chuckled. "How can anyone waste words? It's not like there's only a set amount."

Worser fell silent, annoyed that she had a point.

"Oh, you," his aunt chided. "You remind me of Constance."

He was so fascinated by her statement that he let go of his anger. "Do you mean the way she used to be?" he asked, searching his aunt's face.

"In a way. She used to be so...fixed." Aunt Iris settled on the end of his bed and absently plucked cat hairs off her skirt. "Her light has changed. It's brighter now, unfiltered. I think she smiles more often."

Worser had also noticed that but didn't want to say so. He didn't like the notion that his mother could be happier now. "Sometimes I don't recognize her," he said. "She's changed so much."

Aunt Iris lifted her hand toward him, then stopped and instead began smoothing the rumples in his gray bedspread. "We're all changing constantly. She just happened to change more drastically and abruptly than people usually do."

Worser considered this. He felt suddenly weary but resisted the urge to sit down beside her.

"The thing is," Aunt Iris went on, closing her eyes, "I thought I'd never get to spend quality time with your mother again. You know how it was back before. She and I would visit now and then, have polite chit-chat, maybe exchange birthday gifts and such, but we'd never share real, honest moments. Not like we did as girls. Somehow we lost our spiritual connection."

The phrase *spiritual connection* conjured an image of cloud-like power lines, and Worser almost let out a mocking snort. But he didn't—or couldn't. His insides felt wobbly.

It was true that beyond work, his mother didn't have time for others—except him. Lately, though, he saw the foolishness in that approach. There's a critical flaw to limiting a social circle to two: if one of the pair leaves, the other ends up completely alone.

"She is getting better, right?" Worser asked.

Aunt Iris's eyes slowly found his. "Of course she is!" She leaped to her feet. "Enough of this moping. Like I said, we'd like to spend time with you, Potato. So, what should we do? Tell me, what are you thinking in that potato head of yours?"

"Nothing," he mumbled, annoyed with the question, but then, an idea popped into his mind. "Actually...," he added, "I was thinking that I might go to the library to research advertising."

"Advertising?"

"For...a project. Could you take me?"

Aunt Iris grinned impishly. "Are you saying you could use my help after all?"

Worser's cheeks burned. He had to give his aunt credit for her arguing skills. She wasn't in the same warrior class as his mother, who could slay with one or two perfectly crafted verbal lashes. Instead, Aunt Iris was stealthy—like a sniper. Able to wait things out and seek the perfect angles.

"I'm just teasing you," she said with a giggle. "I'll gladly take you to the library...on one condition. First, I want to you to do something for me. Something that will get you out of this sad, stuffy room."

"But that's bribery."

"Oh, hogwash. I'm not your hired driver. It's perfectly reasonable for me to ask a favor in return. Do we have a deal?"

"I don't know what to do."

"Just paint."

"Paint what?"

"Anything—or nothing in particular. Just put color on the canvas."

Worser had on one of his aunt's homemade towel-smocks and was standing before an easel. As he stared at the vast rectangle of white, he felt daunted and disoriented. He imagined he would have the same reaction if someone had plopped him into the cockpit of a helicopter and told him to take it for a spin.

"You saw your mother's beautiful picture, right?" Aunt Iris stood off to the side, coaching him. "That's her expressing herself, and you can do the same. All you have to do is paint whatever you have in your head."

"I can't. The only things in my head are words."

"All right, fine. I'll give you something to paint." Aunt Iris disappeared for several seconds and returned with a cluster of gerbera daisies in a clay urn. "There. Paint that," she said, setting them on the nearby credenza.

"This is such nonsense. You're doing this to humiliate me, aren't you?"

"I only want you to step outside yourself for a while. To let go of the words banging around in that head of yours."

Worser resisted the urge to toss the paintbrush at her. "Why do you keep insisting that spoken or written communication doesn't matter? Language is what sets us apart.

Without language, we'd be as simple and passive as...as those daisies."

"Those daisies are anything *but* simple or passive," she said, turning the urn and adjusting the flowers just so. "They consume light, convert carbon dioxide into oxygen, and attract bees to spread their pollen. Plus, many scientists think they do, in fact, communicate—by smell."

Worser scoffed. The thought that smells could impart the same nuance and complexity as human language was preposterous.

"Just one picture. That's all. And I'm your chauffeur to the library and back. It's a fair trade, don't you agree?"

Worser did not agree, but he had no choice except to give in. With a final groan, he dipped his brush into the brown and began to paint. At first it was onerous and frustrating. His lines were too thick, his colors bled together, and there were all sorts of spatters and renegade drips. Aunt Iris sat in lotus position on the floor nearby, advising him not to press too hard, to lighten up on the amount of paint, and to angle his brush for different results.

Gradually, he lost himself in his task. Aunt Iris grew silent. And before him, a crude image began to emerge out of paint splotches.

After one last dab of yellow, he stepped back. To his astonishment, the picture wasn't laughable. In fact, it made him smile. The choppy lines added to the charm of the piece. It did look rather like daisies in an urn—if viewed through the bumpy glass of the shower door. Painting was nothing like the heady rush he got when writing for his Masterwork, but he could almost grasp why his aunt loved doing it.

"Oh my." Aunt Iris was standing next to him. "I like this very much. Do you have a title for it?"

Worser nodded. *"Daisies Lack Lackadaisical Days."*

At the library, the books on advertising were useless. Every example seemed to require immense amounts of time and skills Worser didn't possess. Nothing seemed designed for a modest store selling used books in a nondescript shopping center in a small southwestern college town.

At least his mother seemed to be enjoying herself. He watched as she moved through the library in that careful, plodding walk she now had. She ran her hands over book covers, thumped a few thick reference guides as if they were drums, and even held a magazine to her cheek—she did everything except open to a page and read.

His aunt disappeared into the stacks for a while, and later he saw her at the circulation desk with a couple of books. Worser couldn't see the titles before she slipped them into her woven bag. But considering she'd been in the nonfiction section with him, he imagined they weren't novels. Probably books on art. Or cats. Or carpeting.

"How were you able to check those out?" he asked as she joined him in the Dewey Decimal 600s section.

"On Constance's card," she explained.

Worser was aghast. "But that's fraud," he said. "It's practically identity theft!"

Aunt Iris shrugged. "Yes, I suppose it isn't completely honest. But my own library is an hour away, and to get my own card here I'd have to make this my permanent address."

Worser bit his tongue. Claiming his home as her own would be a far more serious transgression.

"We really need to get going. We don't want to wear Constance out." She gestured to where his mother sat droopily in a padded chair in the reference section. "Did you find what you needed?"

"No."

"That's too bad. What about your project?"

"I'll figure something else out."

"I'm sure you will."

The three of them piled back into the Volkswagen, and his aunt pulled the car onto the street. As she drove, she began to sing along to the radio in her high, flute-like voice. It was all nonsense syllables—*la la la*s, and *ba dee bum*s, some fast, some slow, some with trills. Worser sank into the back seat and tried his best to bear it.

"Don't you ever learn the lyrics?" he asked.

Aunt Iris laughed. "I just like the melody. Would you like me to sing something with lyrics I know?"

"It doesn't matter," he replied. And it was true. Either way, it would annoy him.

"*La la la laaa la-la,*" she started up again.

Seconds later, Worser heard something else—something astonishing. His mother was singing along. Her syllables were all *ba ba ba*s and *be be be*s, but it was the same tune.

It was the first time he had ever heard her sing.

Aunt Iris shared a glance with him in the rearview mirror. Her smile revealed that she'd heard this before from his mother, and Worser felt a twinge of envy amid all the wonder.

After a few minutes, his aunt turned down the radio and said, "You know, I'm sure you're both as hungry as I am. Instead of going straight home and waiting for me to cook a meal, how about we find a nice place to eat out?"

Worser studied his mother's profile. "Mom is rather selective about her restaurants. There are only three that she deems worth the effort."

"Oh? Would you like to go to one of them?"

Worser nodded and recommended Kim Phung, their favorite eatery.

Aunt Iris pulled over to look up the address on her cell phone and discovered it was close by. "Well then," she said. "It was written in the stars."

Worser suggested his mother have her usual moo goo gai pan, but after consulting the menu with Aunt Iris, his mother kept pointing at the photo of the yellow curry. So Aunt Iris ordered a bowl for her, without rice, and cut up the biggest chunks of meat before giving it to her. Worser fretted that his mother would leave with regrets, tongue burns, and hunger pangs, but she didn't. She ate almost the entire bowl via her slow, careful spoonfuls—more than usual for her evening meal since the stroke—with gusto even.

It was yet another change in her. Discovering such changes, it seemed, was the only constant in his life. He did notice how much better she'd gotten at using a spoon, though. Her movements were smoother, more precise, and there was very little mess. That was a good thing.

Later, as he lay on his bed, he reviewed the events of the day again in his mind. The costume had been a fiasco and his library research went nowhere, but his mother had seemed in high spirits. She'd even sung and enjoyed her dinner.

"It was written in the stars," his aunt had said.

Worser suddenly bolted upright and threw back his covers, jettisoning Seer, who had been hidden among the folds.

He had thought of the perfect way to publicize the store,

a way that wouldn't disturb Mr. Murray or even require Herbie's help.

All he needed was his bank card.

As much as he didn't want to wait, Worser felt that the next Saturday would be the best day for his big advertising endeavor. He'd researched options, planned it all out, and made the arrangements by phone. The only person he told was Herbie.

On Thursday evening, he worried many times that Herbie might tell Lit Club about their upcoming publicity stunt—and the reason for it. Especially since the meeting was a bit of a dud. As promised, the group didn't help Worser with his Masterwork. He told them he'd forgotten to bring it—which was a ridiculous lie since he always had it on him—and that he wasn't making new entries. He also feigned a headache so that he couldn't lead them in any word games. This seemed to please Donya, but the resulting analysis of two more anonymous submissions was lackluster, and the meeting adjourned early. Donya's friend Anonymous hadn't shown, but that was probably for the best since the evening had been so dull. Also, the nicest comment anyone had about the new lyrics was courtesy of Felicity, who said, "It rhymes in places."

At long last, it was Saturday, the day of Worser's grand plan—the day he would save Re-Visions.

At 10:00 a.m., Worser stood in Herbie's shadow in the parking lot, staring overhead. Finally, he saw it. A silver prop plane was cutting through the sky above, droning happily like a bumblebee.

"Is that it?" Herbie asked.

"I'm sure it is." Worser stood on his tiptoes, out of excitement and a futile effort to get closer to the plane.

Unlike the Saturday before, it was cooler and breezier, and the people out engaging in the day's activities seemed more upright and alert. Even the jack-o'-lanterns decorating many of the plaza's shop windows seemed to be grinning happily at him. Worser congratulated himself on finding the perfect solution to his problem.

He and Herbie stood at attention, looking like saluting soldiers as they used their hands to shield their eyes from the sun's glare.

"Whoa!" Herbie exclaimed.

As they watched, the little plane began to emit a billowy white line. Then it looped and dived, and added to the line, to make an *R* shape.

"Here it goes!" Worser was bouncing on his feet.

R-E-V-I-S the plane wrote.

"Almost done! Let's go get Mr. Murray!" Herbie said.

Together they tore into the store, talking simultaneously. Before the poor man knew what was happening, he was being pulled outside to a median in the parking lot.

"Look!" Worser said, pointing toward the sky. "Look what it says!"

Mr. Murray squinted. "Kinda looks like...*REVISIONS*."

"Of course it does!" Worser said, feeling insulted. He shielded his eyes and peered up—and was alarmed to see that the once-perfect letters were now warping and stretching beyond recognition. "Oh no."

The man on the phone had said something about this—about wind conditions and other factors out of his control. And no refunds. But Worser had assumed the letters would stay legible long enough to make a difference.

He scanned the vicinity. Surely others saw it. Surely his

efforts had created some stir among the potential customers. But it seemed as though no one else had noticed. As he should have remembered, people rarely looked up.

Undeterred, Worser waved his hand to get the attention of a woman walking past. "Excuse me," he said. "Do you see that sign overhead in the sky?"

The woman looked at him, completely baffled, and finally gazed upward. "Oh yeah. Look at that."

"Can you tell what it says?"

"Hmm... *RAISINS*? Yeah. I think that's it." She turned toward him and shrugged. "Probably some store is having a sale on raisins."

"But..." Worser's gears seem to lock up. For a moment, he could only stand there, mouth slightly agape. "Why would a grocery store do that?" he said finally. Except the woman was already out of earshot.

"Don't worry, kid," Mr. Murray said. "At least you're getting the word out about eating more fiber. Now, if you'll excuse me."

The boys watched as he loped back to the store.

Worser sank down onto the curb and buried his face in his hands. His perfect plan was blown—rather literally. He was down $6,000 in his bank account and had nothing to show for it.

"Now it looks kind of like *PRISONS*," Herbie mused. A moment later he added, "Now it looks kind of like *BACONS*."

Herbie kept up his unhelpful commentary for a good ten minutes until Worser stood and clapped the dirt off the seat of his pants.

"All right," he said. "It's time to tell the rest of the club."

SIXTEEN

Admission

"The bookstore might have to close."

"And my monkey suit didn't work."

"*Gorilla* suit, Herbie. It was a gorilla costume."

The other Lit Club members sat gazing at Worser and Herbie. They looked like dogs do when they hear a strange noise. Heads tilted. Brows furrowed. Muscles tensed as if ready to bolt for the nearest exit. Worser had told them there was bad news, but as he stood facing them, he found that explaining the unfortunate turn of events proved even more difficult than he'd anticipated. He had been their savior when he arranged to have them meet there—and now he was letting them down.

Mr. Murray stepped forward from where he'd been listening in from the other side of a bookcase. "Look, what these fellas are trying to say is that my rent is going up, I can't pay it, store will close, end of story."

It hurt Worser's heart to see the group stiffen and glance at one another with wide, worried eyes.

"Isn't there something we can do?" Donya asked.

"We've been trying, but it's hard," Herbie said. "I passed out."

Worser was regretting taking Herbie up on his offer to help divulge the bad news. But of course, it wouldn't have been any easier on his own.

"Guys, I appreciate the fuss, but I've accepted my fate," Mr. Murray said. "Sometimes you gotta know when to move on." He gave a helpless shrug. For four long seconds, he gazed sadly at the group. Then he lifted his hand in a half-waving, half-shoving motion. "Like now. I'm moving on to the sales counter, and I want quiet back here."

Once he was gone, Worser and Herbie sank into their chairs. The group sat silently, each person staring down miserably at the old, scratched-up table.

Felicity was the first to speak, slowly at first, and in a lower, more somber key than was typical for her. "So...why don't we just take turns meeting at each other's houses?"

"No. No way." Donya shook her head vigorously. "I've done that with other stuff, and it's hideous. I hate it. We deserve our own space—a neutral space."

"Maybe we could increase business by luring people here?" Lee said.

Mae laughed derisively. "Didn't Worser and Herbie try that? Maybe we could use a trail of candy."

Lee sighed. "I mean, why not just offer up something in the store that no one can resist."

"Like...books?" Worser gestured around the shop.

"*In addition* to books."

"Ohhh." Herbie nodded. "Like a bonus for coming in."

"Right," Lee said, nodding at Herbie. "So, what's a thing that everyone likes?"

"Nachos?" Herbie suggested.

"Smartphones," Mae said.

"Kittens!" Felicity called out.

"School holidays," Donya mumbled.

Lee shook his head. "Something more universal," he said. "Something adults like as much as kids."

Felicity spun around in her seat. "Mr. Murray!" she shouted out. "What's something that you really like?"

"Peace and quiet," came the reply.

"I don't think quiet is universally loved," Herbie said, tapping the side of his chin. "Lots of people like to listen to stuff."

"Music," Mae mumbled.

"What?" Lee asked.

"I said"—Mae turned toward Lee—"people like music."

"That's true." Donya sat up straight and glanced around the shop. "What if we had music here? Like...a small concert? If we did that a few times, it would bring people in and maybe get the word out about the store."

"I'm not sure Mr. Murray would do that," Lee said.

"Besides, how would it work?" Felicity asked. "There isn't enough room."

"There is in back," Herbie said.

Mae looked confused. "In back?"

"We cleaned out the storage room," Herbie said. "It might work."

Suddenly Donya was on her feet, her eyes shining. "Show us."

There was much screeching and chatting as everyone pushed back their chairs and tramped toward the sales counter. By the time they arrived, Mr. Murray already looked miserable.

Worser said, "Mr. Murray? Could we look in the storage room?" He braced himself for griping.

To his surprise, Mr. Murray muttered, "Knock yourself out. It's unlocked."

The small crowd ambled behind Herbie as he strode into the dark storage area. Worser switched on a light and, for some reason, a couple of them went "Oooh." The room did seem much bigger now that the only things in it were the wooden folding chairs, the few remaining plastic bins, and the pile of Bubble Wrap.

"It used to be full of boxes," Herbie said.

Donya was walking in a wide circle, glancing around the room. After a complete loop she nodded and headed back into the shop. The others followed.

"I think it might work," Donya said. She wore one of her loveliest grins—one of Worser's favorites—giddy and a tad devious.

"Are you sure it's big enough?" Mae asked. "Does it have everything we'd need?"

Donya shrugged. "No idea. But I know someone we can ask. Hang on a sec."

She was out the front door in an instant. The group watched as she paced up and down the sidewalk, talking on her cell phone.

Eventually she headed back inside. "Success!" she said, waving her phone. "He'll be here as soon as he can."

"Yay!" Felicity shouted.

The whole club was smiling, except Worser.

He didn't like music.

He didn't like the thought of handing their fate over to a stranger.

And he really didn't like that Donya had said *he*.

"Wait just a minute." Mr. Murray raised his hands. "Would one of you mind telling me what's going on?"

"I promise we will," Donya said. "As soon as we know more. Luckily, help is on the way."

"Dudes. You guys look super low. Hope I can ease the suffrage."

Suffering! Worser yelled inside his head.

The "help," it turned out, was Turk. As soon as Worser saw the familiar lanky shape pulling up on a cruiser bike with blinking red lights, the rider's shaggy hair poking out from beneath a shiny black helmet, his already gloomy mood turned funereal. He hoped a fellow Lit Club member would point out—or even laugh at—Turk's grand mistakes with vocabulary, but no one did. In fact, Felicity started to follow Turk, puppy-like, around the storage room.

"What instrument do you play?"

"Bass."

"Nice. I play flute—and a little bit of the piccolo, but we don't use that much in band. Are you in band at school?"

"No."

"Who taught you to play?"

"I taught myself."

"Wow. You must have natural talent."

Turk checked out the platform in the back of the room, inspecting the holes where, at one time, a counter must have been.

"What do you think?" Donya asked, stepping out of the knot of onlookers.

"Cool space. Good acoustics."

"Could you play here?"

"Think so. Might get hot in here with a crowd. The riser has some roughage along the front, but it can hold us." He grinned at them. "I'm game."

Herbie cheered. Lee said, "Yes!" Felicity squealed. And Mae pumped her fist.

Donya pressed her hands together as if in prayer. "Thank you," she said in a velvety tone.

"No problemo. But"—Turk made a halt gesture—"I gotta ask the bandmates first."

"I get it," Donya said. "We still need to ask Mr. Murray, too."

"What's the name of your band?" Mae asked Turk.

"Don't know. We were called Male Strum, but then Janine joined us and vetoed it. We haven't thought of a new one yet."

"You would need a name when we advertise the concert," Lee said. "If you do the concert, that is."

"Ooh!" Felicity's hand shot up as if she were sitting in the front of a class. "Maybe a name that makes people think of books *and* music!"

Turk laughed. "What name would do that?"

"*Volume.*" Worser pursed his lips. The term had popped into his head, and he'd uttered it without thinking.

"*Volume*..." Turk was nodding. "The Volumes."

"Nice," Felicity said, and others added murmurs of approval.

"Not bad." Turk gave one last decisive nod. "Thanks, Library Boy."

"Why do you call him Library Boy?" Herbie asked.

Turk grinned. "That's just our thing."

Herbie nodded as if he understood—which he couldn't have.

Turk explained that he needed to step out into the parking lot and call the rest of his band. Meanwhile, the club members began chatting excitedly—all except Donya, who drifted to the front of the store. Worser followed and found her standing at the window, watching Turk on his phone.

She started when she saw Worser standing beside her. "Oh! You scared me."

"Sorry." Worser watched her gaze return to Turk. "How do you know him so well?"

"Turk?" Donya smiled shyly. "I've been tutoring him a couple of times a week after school."

"I didn't know that."

"It just started this year. We were supposed to meet in the library, but, you know, Ludlum closed it, so we started having sessions at Regular Jo's."

Worser had heard of that place—a known hangout for students. But it hadn't met his mother's standards, so he'd never been there.

"The idea that you two would be friends is... is incongruous. He's a thug."

Donya laughed. "No he's not. I mean, I know he gets in trouble at school a lot, but he's really sweet, actually. And smart."

Worser resisted the impulse to roll his eyes.

It flummoxed him why she would consider Turk intelligent. Not fifteen minutes earlier, the man-boy had confused *suffrage* with *suffering*—basically saying he wanted to relieve them of their voting rights.

"He's Anonymous, isn't he?"

She nodded. "He wants to get better with his writing. He loves words, just like you."

Worser's self-control failed, and he laughed a big snorting laugh.

"It's *true*," Donya said, fixing him with a fierce glare. "Except he doesn't just play with words, like some people. Instead of making lists, he makes people feel things."

"Nauseous, for instance?"

Donya turned from the window and glared directly at Worser. "You're a stuck-up know-it-all!"

Worser recoiled as if he'd been slapped. It hurt that she'd admire the writing of someone clearly inferior. "I'm only concerned about your lapse in judgment."

"You don't know him," she said through her teeth. "And you don't know me, either."

"That's absurd. Of course I know you. We met when we were preschoolers."

"That may be. But it's not like we're friends." With that, she stomped away from Worser, out through the door, and in the direction of Turk.

Ten minutes later Turk reentered the store with Donya, announcing that The Volumes were, as he put it, "all in." The club members, who had joined Worser at the front window, clapped and cheered. Donya practically gleamed with happiness, which was very hard for Worser to witness. He returned to his spot at the meeting table, away from the celebration and any withering looks Donya might be shooting him.

Worser half hoped that Mr. Murray would quash the idea of a concert, and half hoped he wouldn't, since he knew it was their best marketing idea yet. Now sitting far away, he also only half heard Donya as she made her case to the store owner.

At first, she kept her voice soft and even-toned—no doubt to appeal to Mr. Murray's love of quiet. But as she went on, her speech grew louder and clearer. Her line of reasoning sounded well thought-out. It would be a free event, just for publicity. The Lit Club would do all the setup and cleanup. They could use the rear door of the storage room as a concert entrance, and keep the door leading to the shop open so that people could buy things. They would limit the number of attendees—should they need to—so as not to break fire code. Guests could use the bathroom, and club members would clean it when the show was over. Mr. Murray would only have to agree to one concert now, but hopefully it would be a smashing success and they could do more.

Meanwhile, Worser, still jumbled with conflicting emotions, tried to distract himself by writing a Masterwork entry titled "The Lost Ins and Outs." He managed one whimsical line (*Are outlaws the opposite of in-laws?*), but soon his frustration began to seep into his work. (*Guess who dropped in? Turk, the future dropout.*) Eventually, it deteriorated into a pseudo-literary rant about Turk. (*Turk plays bass. Bass, pronounced differently, is also a fish. But Turk is inferior to even fish. He is beneath them. He is, therefore, a bass-turd.*)

"What have you got to lose?" Donya's rising plea to Mr. Murray broke through his thoughts.

"You mean besides my temper? My peace of mind?" came Mr. Murray's gruff reply. There followed a long pause and then, "Fine. Whatever. Just don't expect me to do anything. Maybe it will help me clear out the stock."

"Oh, thank you!"

Worser heard more sounds of rejoicing, a few low mutterings from Mr. Murray, and the thumps, chatter, jingling of the door bells, and cries of "Bye, Worser!" as people left. Then silence.

Evidence suggested the concert was on, and Worser's reaction was a resounding, though unvoiced, *hooray/harrumph!* He was glad for the hope this endeavor provided, but he also felt somewhat invaded. Outshone. Insecure. Out of whack.

"Hey, kid. You still here?" Mr. Murray stood at the opposite end of the table.

"Obviously."

"How come you're here so much? Don't you have your own place to go to?"

"I'm not out on the street or anything. I have a home." He was trying for a glib tone, but the word *home* caught in his throat.

"Well, that's good to hear. So why aren't you there?"

"It's...complicated."

"Homes usually are."

Worser waited, but Mr. Murray stayed put. He seemed to expect more of an answer.

"It's my mom. She's—" Worser broke off. He found that beyond his reluctance to speak about his situation, he also had trouble finding the right words—which he might have considered fitting, almost poetic, if he hadn't felt so sad. "She's gone."

"She died?"

"No, she didn't die. She...went away."

"Ah. Sorry, kid. My old man took off when I was about your age. It's a lousy thing to do to a kid, that's for sure. Makes you feel like you can't count on anybody. Like everyone's just out for themselves."

Worser had no idea how to explain that his mother was still around and in his house. That he saw her every day, and yet he also hadn't seen her in months. It was an enigma—emphasis on *ma*.

"Anyway, I'm closing up for the night." Mr. Murray began folding the chairs. "Sorry, kid. Time for you to say goodbye."

SEVENTEEN

Storm

Lee designed flyers for The Volumes' concert. Felicity told her friends in band class. Herbie submitted info to an online events calendar. Donya targeted the adult demographic, roping in her father to spread the word and hang up flyers at the university. Mae even paid five bucks to the kid who read morning announcements, asking him to put in a quick plug—and said the resulting lunch detention was worth it. Thursday's meeting was spent going over checklists and assigning new tasks.

Worser knew he should be pleased—after all, this was what he'd wanted: a viable attempt at saving the store. But he wasn't pleased at all. Or happy. Or content. Or satisfied. Or in any way cheerful.

Now, with the store at risk, every part of his life hung in the balance. He felt unsteady and jittery—at times a bit seasick.

His rocky state had increased by the day. And then, suddenly, he awoke to find it was Friday, the day before the concert. Just thirty-two hours to go.

Downstairs his aunt was zooming about the kitchen in a

faster, more frenetic state than usual, talking to herself the entire time.

"I thought I put the...? Oh yes, here it is. And the...? Right. I left it over there. Oh, why didn't I...? Good heavens, Iris, you can't forget...Mercy me! Look at the time!"

Worser stood at the dining room threshold, safely out of harm's way. "Why are you making such a commotion?" he asked. "You're going to wake up Mom."

"She's up. She's ready. I'm the one who can't find a tree in a forest. But we'll be on our way in just a minute." She pulled a pen out of her hair and made a check mark on a small handwritten list.

"What on earth are you talking about?"

"The appointment!" She pointed over his head at the wall calendar. "It's today."

Right. It seemed impossible he would have forgotten his mother's assessment with the neurologist—and yet he had. The turmoil over the concert had caused him to lose track of days.

"Oh, I meant to tell you!" Aunt Iris did a brisk about-face. "You'll be going home with Donya Khoury after school."

"I...what?"

"That specialist's office is fifty-two miles away, and by the time we're done and back on the road, we'll hit rush hour. Plus, it's supposed to rain, which always causes such a muddle. Anyway"—she paused to take a breath—"Dr. Khoury said you might as well have dinner with them, so he'll be picking up both you and his daughter after school."

"Oh...yes...I suppose that would be all right."

Aunt Iris didn't hear him, as she had already rushed out of the room to fetch his mother. After three trips back and forth from the house to her car, they were loaded up and ready to leave.

"Have fun with the Khourys!" Aunt Iris called as she backed her car out of the driveway. "And don't forget your umbrella!"

By the time final bell rang, the town was being buffeted by a severe thunderstorm. The sky looked like Aunt Iris's murky paint water, and ominous rumblings rattled windows and caused lights to flash on and off.

And, of course, Worser had forgotten the umbrella.

"Want Nanna to drive you home?" Herbie asked. He and Worser stood side by side, staring through the double glass doors leading to the pickup circle, their view partially obstructed by turkey and cornucopia decals.

"I already have a ride," Worser explained. "I think I'm supposed to meet them here."

"Okay. I'll see you tomorrow at the concert." Herbie's statement coincided with a deep growl from the heavens. "Bye!"

Worser watched Herbie bound down the sidewalk through the rain. The scene outdoors was a complete mess. People were rushing to buses and cars. Others stood in clusters under the covered entrance to the school, some screeching delightedly with every thunder crack. Muddy water splashed over everything.

And there was no Dunya in sight.

Eventually, he recognized a green Volvo crawling along the curb at the pickup circle—the Khourys' Frog. He scurried toward it.

"Hello, William," Dr. Khoury greeted as Worser jumped

into the back seat behind Seth, who was riding shotgun. "Awful weather, isn't it?"

"Yes."

"Dude! There was lightning all over on our way here." Seth imitated explosion sounds while jabbing his finger through the air. "It was super cool."

Dr. Khoury craned his neck to better see through the front windshield. "Where's Donya?"

"I don't know."

"Well, I can't stay here and block traffic. I'll try to park close by, where she can find us."

He eased the car into a first-row spot and shut off the engine. There, the three of them sat in the metal-and-glass bubble, listening to the roar of the rain. Dr. Khoury checked his watch and tapped his hands on the steering wheel. Seth watched for lightning.

After several minutes of waiting, Dr. Khoury made a call. "I don't understand where she could be," he remarked, setting down the phone. "Her cell goes straight to voice mail."

"Maybe she forgot to turn it back on at the end of the school day," Worser suggested.

"Perhaps."

Two more minutes passed.

"This isn't like Donya." Dr. Khoury looked worried. "Do you think she might be in the office?"

"I'll go check." Worser headed back toward the school, leaping over puddles as best as he could and missing occasionally.

He was just about to head through the main entrance when a flash of green caught his eye—Donya's hoodie. A corner of it was flapping in the breeze just around the side of the building. Training his sights on the fluttering piece of fabric, he cut a path down the sidewalk into a narrow inlet between the main building and auditorium.

He was right: it was Donya. She was under the eaves, safely out of the rain.

Relief came over him, followed by a series of observations. The first was that she'd chosen an illogical place to stay dry. It would have been far better to stay close to the front door, where there was a roof over the entrance. The second was that her arms had sleeves that didn't match her hoodie, and they seemed abnormally bent across her back. The third was that those arms didn't belong to her at all.

It had taken him a moment to see in the shadowy light that Donya wasn't alone.

"Library Boy?"

Turk was with her. They were standing in each other's embrace—and it was clear now, even to Worser, that they were a couple.

"There you are!" Dr. Khoury sang out when they climbed into the car.

"Sorry. I lost track of time. I was, um…" Donya's ears and cheeks were the color of a pomegranate. "I was just finishing up something for tomorrow." She looked at Worser and warned him with wide, imploring eyes.

"Oh? For the concert?" Dr. Khoury didn't seem to pick up on Donya's stammering and ripening shade. He eased the Volvo out of the parking space and headed toward the lot exit. "How are things going? Are you all ready?"

Donya nodded. "Yup. Mm-hmm."

Worser said nothing. He was finding it difficult to follow the conversation, or even stay in his seat. The storm outside now seemed less foreboding than the conditions inside the car.

He couldn't shake the image of Donya and Turk. Seeing it had felt like a collapse—an upending. He was falling down a rabbit hole, tumbling about in a cyclone, swooping through a sky, coughing up pixie dust, and wearing only his pajamas. He knew, when he landed, that he'd be far away from everything familiar and safe. It had happened to him before.

"I need to go home," he rasped.

"What?" Dr. Khoury glanced at him in the rearview mirror. "William, you're coming home with us. Don't you remember?"

"I need to go home!" Worser's voice was a ragged cry of pain. "I have to!"

Seth turned around to gape at him. "Dude? You feel okay?"

"Leave him alone, Seth," Donya warned.

"Dad, I think Worser's sick. He looks crappy."

"Don't say *crappy*, Seth." Dr. Khoury was finding it difficult to both listen and drive through the torrent of rain. "William, if you don't feel well, why don't you come with us and—"

"Please take me home!"

"All right. All right. We'll do that, then."

Worser wanted to curl up like a wounded animal. It was too much. The debilitating memory on repeat. Seth and Dr. Khoury sneaking looks of pity at him. Donya, beside him, fidgeting guiltily.

The second the Volvo pulled its front tires into Worser's

driveway, he was out of the car and running for the house. Quick as possible, he unlocked the door, raced inside, then locked it again in case anyone tried to follow. Throwing off his backpack, he staggered into the living room and let out a howl of anguish.

In front of him was a violet-painted p-ohm. Still feeling an overwhelming urge to hide, he crawled inside the box and lay there, sobbing. He wept for an unknowable amount of time, soaking the lavender cushion with his tears and wet clothes. Gradually, his cries quieted to whimpers and shudders. It was strangely comforting being in the silence and stillness, with nothing around him but dark blurs.

His weary haze was interrupted by the awareness of something sliding past him. Wiping his eyes, he could see Ging, poking her way through the crate to a dry corner. She curled up and blinked at him, her gaze soft and understanding.

The last thing Worser noticed before falling asleep was a word painted in silver on the wall above the cat.

Love.

His aunt's hand was on his calf, gently shaking him awake. "Potato? We're home."

It took Worser a moment to come to—to remember. When he finally did, he wanted only to fall back to sleep, to avoid everything and everyone.

"Come on out and eat something. Get into some dry clothes."

The fact that she wasn't bombarding him with questions could mean only one thing: Dr. Khoury had already told her about his outburst, and about his wanting to go home instead.

"Come on, Potato."

As much as he wanted to shun the world, he couldn't push away the fact that he was cold, hungry, and kind of itchy. Slowly and achily, he pulled himself onto his hands and knees and began backing out of the crate. Ging, he noticed, was no longer there. Had he imagined her?

"There's some clean laundry in that basket. Find yourself some pajamas and get changed while I make you some hot tea and a sandwich."

For the first time since that morning, Worser looked at his aunt. She looked haggard after the long day. Her features hung lower on her face, and her movements had very little lift to them.

He found his forest-green sweatpants and put them on in the downstairs bathroom, reveling in their dryness and clean fragrance. Afterward, he peeked through the doorway to his mom's room and saw that she was fast asleep, her right hand drooping just over the edge of the bed, as if asking to be held. He considered tucking it back under the covers, but he gently shut the door instead.

When he returned to the table, Aunt Iris was just setting a toasted-cheese-and-tomato sandwich in front of his chair. He sat down and slowly began eating.

"I suppose you're eager to hear how it went," she said.

He wasn't, mainly because he couldn't feel much of anything. He had gone numb from exposure—not to the elements, but to the horrifying truth about Donya and Turk. Now, as he remembered the appointment, curiosity returned. He set down his sandwich and looked expectantly at his aunt.

"The doctor's news was...not what we'd hoped." Her voice wavered. "Don't you worry. Your mom's getting better.

She is. It's just going to take longer than we expected for her to really improve."

"What—" Having not spoken in hours, Worser at first could only manage a croak. "What are you saying?"

"I'm saying her recovery is probably going to take years, not months, and there are important steps we need to take."

"Years?" Worser shook his head slowly. "No. That's not right. She's been working so hard. You kept saying it wouldn't be long."

"I know. I'm sorry. I should never have said that. I just..." Aunt Iris stared out the kitchen window. The storm had passed, leaving behind darkness and a steady, melancholy drip from the edge of the roof. "In the hospital they said a long recovery time was likely, but that sometimes it happened more quickly. I chose to focus on the best possible scenario. I wanted to believe it, and I wanted you to believe it. I guess I thought that our faith might somehow help the outcome."

For a moment, Worser couldn't speak. He was still stuck on the word *years*, almost as if he were hearing it for the first time. What did it mean? It had the letter *y*—like *yearn* and *yesterday*. Followed by *ears*, which was where it was stuck echoing, unable to penetrate his mind.

He shook his head, trying to dislodge both the word and the concept. "You're just being dramatic. Surely there's a solution. We can hire more doctors. Or different ones. Or..." His voice trailed off. Again, words seemed strange and out of reach.

"No. We just have to keep on doing what we've been doing." Aunt Iris stood to answer the whistling kettle. "The doctor was pleased to hear about her care. It helps being surrounded by loved ones, you know." She handed him a cup with a tea bag floating in it, set down one for herself, and took her seat again.

Worser watched as a murky dark cloud emanated from the tea bag, slowly overtaking the water in the cup.

"There's just one more thing." Aunt Iris's pitch rose ever so slightly, and she nervously twirled a spoon between her fingers. "It has been advised that I get power of attorney over your affairs."

"What?" Worser's face grew cold.

"It's simply a formality. I've been looking into the matter, just in case." She attempted a smile. "It won't be hard at all."

The whole world seemed to tilt, and Worser gripped the edge of the table. "You've been...looking into this?" he repeated. "You've been planning this?"

Worry crept into his aunt's face as she caught sight of Worser's shocked expression. "I just did some reading. I wanted to be ready, in case I needed to step in."

"Step in as what? *My mother?*" Worser's chest heaved. "You're *not* my mother."

"Of course I'm not. I never could be. It's just...this is for the best."

"For whom? Admit it. It's best for *you*." His words came out on hot, ragged breaths. There was fiery heat within him, but a jittery chill on the outside. Anger inside fear. *Fanger.*

"Best for me?" Aunt Iris was shaking her head. "How?"

"You're happy this happened to her!"

His aunt gasped. "How can you say such a thing?"

"You like her better now that she's different."

"Potato, I—"

"Stop calling me that!"

Aunt Iris closed her eyes and began her deep, stress-relief

breathing. The sight infuriated him. He wanted her to be stressed. He wanted her to hurt worse than he did.

"You don't know how to take care of me!" he snapped.

"I've *been* taking care of you!" Aunt Iris's volume and vehemence surprised him. He'd never heard her sound so upset. "I've been looking out for you for eight years!"

"You're lying."

Aunt Iris sat quietly for a moment. "After your father died, it was hard for your mom," she restarted in a shaky voice. "She did her best, but she was suffering. She was so sad."

Worser wanted to continue shouting at her, to tell her she had no clue what she was talking about, but all he could do was sit and seethe about another unsettling twist in his life: *his mother had lost her husband.* He'd known that already, intellectually, but hadn't considered how it affected her.

Worser had very few memories of his father—and what he did recall was patchy and fuzzy. He remembered the shuffling way his dad walked, shoulders back, head stiff—as if he were being pulled forward by his belly. (Worser had inherited this.) He remembered his cough-like laugh and the way he would stroke his beard and go "Hrmm" whenever he was deep in thought. He remembered his brown leather shoes with the pinhole detailing around the edges. He also had a memory of his father shouting "Enough!"—just once, during a disagreement at the dinner table. That was all. Then, one day, he was told his father was gone, and four-year-old Worser learned new important-sounding words like *epitaph* and *eulogy*.

He'd never really wondered about his parents as a couple. It had been just him and his mother for so long that he gave no thought to what his mom and dad must have meant to each other, or how their marriage worked.

But now he was. Now it was as if a fog were being burned from his mind. All these years he'd assumed that he'd been sufficient company for his mother—even when a part of him always sensed that he wasn't.

"It was hard on her," his aunt continued. "Work. The house. You. It was too much, I could tell. She did the best she could, but she was depressed."

Worser shook his head. "Depressed? She was uncompromising. Formidable even."

"Grief can look like that."

Worser stared down at his half-eaten sandwich, feeling dizzy and depleted by the day's events. His aunt, unfortunately, interpreted his silence as acceptance.

"Power of attorney won't mean anything," she said. "It's just a technicality, so I can sign documents for school and other matters. It'll be—"

"ENOUGH!"

Worser stood up so fast, the chair toppled over backward. He made no effort to pick it up.

What would be the point? Nothing was as it should be.

EIGHTEEN

Loss

Worser couldn't fall back into deep sleep after bolting from his aunt. Instead, he thrashed about, achy and fretful—feverish without fever. Or, as he reflected, he *spent the rest of his rest in a state of unrest.*

By late morning, he remained sprawled on his bed, his mind a heap of rubble. Ging had come in at some point and curled into a doughnut shape between his feet. As daylight illuminated his room, he saw that Seer was there, too, sitting on the floor beside the bed, watching with apparent curiosity. Worser found himself feeling bad for the two animals and the change they must have endured—snatched from the great outdoors to his aunt's apartment, then torn from that home to this one.

On a whim, Worser stretched out his finger and tapped Seer gently on the nose. The cat seemed to consider this gesture, then nuzzled Worser's hand and trotted out the half-open door.

Worser knew he should follow. He should get up, go downstairs, and go to the bookstore, where The Volumes' concert would begin that afternoon.

He couldn't.

He should.

If he went, he would see Donya again. At this thought, his insides spiraled downward, whirling without release—like a toilet that wouldn't flush.

But he also needed to know how things would unfold. The fate of the bookstore might be determined today, and he felt obligated to see it through. It had meant so much to him these past couple of months—almost as much as Donya.

The Lit Club had scheduled sound check for two o'clock and the concert from three to five—peak business hours on Saturdays at the shopping center. Worser eventually decided he would, in fact, go. He would arrive early, seek out a secluded spot, maybe even work on his Masterwork. But throughout it all, he'd remain as aloof and unseen as possible. Like Ging.

Worser kept to himself until it was time to head to the concert. At one-thirty, he grabbed his backpack, shouted, "I'm leaving now!" from the foyer, and then scurried away as quickly as he could. He took some pride in his clean getaway. Aunt Iris and his mom knew his whereabouts—*Lit Club Event* had been on today's calendar square for over a week, and he'd even announced his departure. No one could accuse him of being guileful or inconsiderate or in need of an attorney-authorized fake mother.

The bells above the door provided an inappropriately cheery greeting upon his arrival at Re-Visions. Once inside, a curious sensation settled over him, as if he were stuck in place, even as he moved about the shop. He felt as much a part of the surroundings as the dust-covered bookcases, and yet, at the same time, not entirely there. A haunt, or an echo.

Mr. Murray glanced up from his usual perch. "Oh, it's you," he said. "I thought you might be another one of those hairy fellas with guitar cases."

"No," Worser replied, even though the answer was apparent. He was bleary and distracted—and a bit queasy from the day-old scones he'd pilfered for his lunch. "Are you going to watch the concert?"

"Not my thing, kid. I've got to mind the store, so I'll stay right here if it's all the same to you."

"It is all the same," Worser babbled. "I appreciate that about you."

Mr. Murray squinted at him. "You okay, kid? Don't take this the wrong way, but you look like you just crawled out of a dungeon."

"I'm merely tired."

"Uh-huh. Then how about you go find the others and let me do my work here."

Worser left Mr. Murray to his paperback and headed down the short corridor behind the counter. The storage room door was propped open. Inside, everything appeared to be all set. Herbie and the others must have moved the bins of "to be saved" items and the boxes of Bubble Wrap, swept—and possibly mopped—the floor, and placed the wooden folding chairs along the walls. On the platform at the far end, Turk and his bandmates, all tall eighth graders, stood in various hunched stances as they set up their equipment.

At the sight of Turk, Worser didn't feel the same pain from the day before, but he felt the memory of it—and knew it could fully reassert itself at any moment. He averted his eyes and decided he'd do better in the back of the shop, writing at the oak table.

But as he turned, Donya was suddenly before him. At first it was too much for his brain: Donya in all her loveliness. Gone was her green hoodie. Instead, she wore a pale yellow dress and an assortment of wooden bangles. Her gaze had a searching quality—the same his mother had often fixed him with lately. He had to look away.

"Hey, Worser."

Worser made a sound like *haw*.

"So, um, thanks. For not saying anything to Dad yesterday."

Worser could only nod. His eyes focused on a point of nothingness over her left shoulder. His insides swilled and spun.

"I'm sorry," she went on, "for putting you in such a bad spot."

He bobbed his head a second time.

"Yeah. So, it's going to be a good show, don't you think?"

Her voice was in a pitch his aunt often used with him, cheery but strained. The resemblance irked him.

"I can't say." Finally, his mind was able to assemble words. "My experience with concerts is limited. I mainly find them to be an inefficient use of one's time."

"Well, I have a good feeling," Donya went on, ignoring his grumbles (also very much like his aunt would). "The gig will be great, people all over will hear about the store, and Mr. Murray won't have to close it."

"I hope so."

"All thanks to Turk." Donya glanced toward the stage. Everything about her softened. Her appearance. Her voice. Her posture.

At the same time, Worser seemed to curdle. His back

stiffened, his expression turned to a glare, and a rough, labored quality entered his breath.

"Hello out there! Welcome to sound check." Turk's amplified voice echoed through the space. "Who wants to hear some tunage?"

A smattering of applause rose up from the small crowd of early arrivals. Donya dashed toward the platform and stood front and center, right underneath Turk. Someone let out a loud, irritating whistle, and Worser turned to see Mae standing nearby, watching the band. Lee and Herbie loped up beside her. A second later, Felicity skipped forward to join them.

"Worser! You're here!" Felicity squealed. "Isn't this the best thing ever?"

"Turk is the absolute coolest," Mae said.

Herbie nodded. "He looks like one of those people in the Jeep commercials."

Worser was horror-struck. The same group of friends who had once held him in such high regard, who had applauded him for arranging their Thursday meet-ups in the store, who had seen the mastery behind his Masterwork—they were now staring in awe at Turk. As if *he* were their hero. First Donya, now them.

"I wonder if he can teach us how to write songs," Lee said, rubbing the fuzz on his chin.

"Oh, that would be awesome!" Mae said. "When my writing is done, I—"

"Why do you always do that?" Worser snapped, interrupting her and surprising everyone, including himself.

Mae frowned. "Do what?"

"You take yourself out of the sentence and put it in passive voice. Instead of saying 'When *I* finish my writing,' you make it sound like the writing will complete itself."

"Uh, okay. Are we having a meeting or something?"

"And *you* need to make your characters do something," he said to Lee. "And you need to move past fourth-grade subject matter," he said to Felicity. "And you," he said, turning toward Herbie. "Why are you even part of this? Do you even write?"

"Ma-a-an." Mae stretched the word to three syllables. "What's gotten into you?"

The question was inaccurate. It had felt as if something burst out of him rather than passed into him.

"Are you feeling okay?" Felicity asked.

Lee studied him. "Your eyes are really red."

"And your face is white," Herbie added. "Like mayonnaise."

No. This wouldn't do at all. He had bombarded them with criticism in a desperate effort to remain leader-like—only now he was being stared at in pity.

And then Worser heard something he was even less prepared for.

"Potato?"

Worser spun about so fast, he was left dizzy. His aunt and mother were standing two yards away. They were actually here, *in* the building—in his getaway place. It was *in*compatible. *In*conceivable. *In*appropriate.

He stalked toward them, simmering. "What on earth are you doing here?"

"Dr. Khoury told me about the concert. What a quaint little place! I can see why you like studying here."

This was terrible. Universes should never collide; otherwise, bad things happened. It was a fundamental law of physics.

His aunt patted his left shoulder. "I hope you're... feeling better?"

Worser ignored the question and flinched at the touch. "Mom shouldn't be here. She won't like it," he scolded, ignoring the grin on his mother's face. "Take her home this instant."

"Oh, don't be silly. She needs to get out and have some fun, and a concert is just the ticket. So few happen early in the day like this."

He scanned the room, taking in the back exit that led to the alley, the band, his fellow club members, his mom and aunt, and the open doorway that revealed the bookshop just beyond. It all looked remote and distorted. And again, he felt oddly removed—as if he'd been photoshopped into the scene.

Another touch on his shoulder. "I feel bad about last night," Aunt Iris was saying. "Perhaps later today we can talk?"

Worser was about to proclaim his opposition to the idea when a terrible noise emanated from the stage. The band was running through a song to test the equipment, and the room reverberated with the smashing of drums, bombitty bass lines, and Turk's howling—though mercifully the sound was too garbled to make out the lyrics.

His aunt clutched her hands together and let out a childlike giggle. His mother, to his complete shock, was also laughing.

It was too much, and Worser felt the familiar instinct to flee. He staggered backward until he found himself in the tiny corridor.

If only he could disappear for a bit, try to refocus his thoughts. He glanced at the door to the alley and saw the Lit Club manning the concert entrance. He craned his neck to peek into the store and saw that Dr. and Mrs. Khoury had just arrived.

Then his eyes landed on another door—the small bathroom across from the storage room entrance.

Perhaps there he could find refuge.

Worser threw down his backpack and began pacing, but it ended up being more of a spinning motion because the bathroom was so small—made even smaller by the stack of plastic bins and Bubble Wrap the club must have moved in there to get them out of the way.

Outside, The Volumes were still attempting a song. Every note rankled him. Every whoop from the audience was like a blow to his chest. The concert that was supposed to save everything was ruining everything in the process.

First his house had been turned upside down, and now the bookstore. It wasn't fair. He wanted to send everyone away, to ring a dismissal bell that would make them all file out of the building and go home.

Wait.

A notion came to him. Small at first. Then swelling outward, filling his head like the clouds that billowed from Aunt Iris's steeping teabags. A *What if...?* that turned into a *But how?*

He could set off the smoke alarm.

If the alarm sounded, perhaps Mr. Murray would be concerned enough to cancel the concert. Turk and Aunt Iris and everyone who didn't belong could go home. He'd have his sanctuary back, and it would buy him time to hit upon the right solution to save the store. One that didn't involve Turk. One that would make Worser the gallant savior.

He remembered that the smoke alarm was right outside

the bathroom, on the ceiling. All he needed to do was create a little bit of smoke and direct it through the narrow opening at the top of the door. That should be enough to trigger it.

He dug through his backpack but found nothing that could start a fire. Then he rummaged through the drawers in the sink vanity and came across a box of matches bearing a Casino Arcadia logo.

He tested a match, worried they might be too old to work, but this one did. As he blew it out, a plan took shape in his mind. He got his Masterwork out of his backpack, snatched a few empty pieces of notebook paper from it, and slipped the rubber band from around his pack of colored pencils. Then he rolled up the paper tightly, fastened it with the rubber band, and carefully propped the finished product upright in the sink basin. Hands trembling, he lit another match and set the top end on fire.

Worser carefully grabbed the other end of the roll and stretched his arm up as high as it could go. A couple of seconds passed, but no alarm sounded. Unfortunately, there wasn't enough smoke being created. Perhaps if he got closer to the door?

What happened next would plague him for years to come. As he stepped forward, he tripped over his Masterwork. To prevent himself from falling, he flung his arms out sideways—and his makeshift torch went flying off into the corner, landing on the pile of Bubble Wrap.

By the time he turned his head toward it, the flame had already spread. There was even one tendril snaking up the wall. A column of black smoke flowed up from the flame, thickening and gathering at the top until it began to spread across the ceiling like ominous fog.

Worser watched, aghast, until the heat and smoke proved too much, and his protective reflexes kicked in.

He burst open the door just as the smoke alarm began to blare. "Fire!" he cried.

Felicity stood in the entrance of the storage room. She caught sight of the flames behind him, and her screams blended with the shrieking of the alarm.

Light, hazy smoke was now filling the air, and people began to rush for the door at the back of the storage room. Worser, in his panic, turned in a circle, searching for his mother. He finally saw her, being helped outside by his aunt. But where was Donya?

"Come on!" Herbie was suddenly next to him. He grabbed Worser by the arm and pulled him toward the exit.

Together, they rushed out the back door and joined the cluster of escapees. Worser felt a huge surge of relief when he saw Donya among them, standing with Felicity, Turk, and the rest of the band. He took a deep breath, relishing the fresher, less smoky air.

"Oh, Potato. Thank goodness." Aunt Iris came up behind him, her arms looped around his mother's. "What a fright."

"Be!" his mother shouted. "Be!" She kept patting his head and back. He could barely register it. He felt so numb.

All around, people gasped, murmured, and traded expressions of disbelief. Worser heard a shout and saw Mae and Lee running down the alley toward them.

"Where were you guys?" Donya asked. "I was looking for you."

"We went around to the parking lot in front of the store," Mae explained. "Your parents are there, Donya. And Mr. Murray. They're all fine."

"But man. The store!" Lee said.

Worser gently broke away from his mother. "Do you think the fire will spread to the books?" he asked.

Lee just shook his head gravely.

"Oh! I think I hear the fire department!" Felicity cried out.

Sure enough, sirens were wailing in the distance. By now, plumes of dark smoke were pouring out of the building's openings and shooting toward the sky, forcing the crowd to move backward.

"Damn!" Mae exclaimed. "I knew today would be exciting, but... Damn."

"I just don't understand," Donya said, her voice tight with emotion. "What happened?"

Tears spilled out of Worser's eyes. "I didn't mean it," he mumbled. "I didn't mean it."

Donya gaped at him. "What?"

He could say no more. He was shaking too hard.

"Oh my god. Worser? What did you do?"

NINETEEN

Limbo

Worser ran.

As he ran, his brain also seemed to be racing. Thoughts darted through like comets, too fast to fully take in. *Fire. Mom. Donya. "What did you do?" The store. Mr. Murray. Fire. My fault. My fault. Mine.*

He was not a savior. He was a destroyer.

As soon as he passed into the familiar wooded area, he felt a small sense of comfort and safety beneath the cover of oaks and cedars. He kept running until he reached his tree and hastily scrambled up.

Perhaps because his movements were jerkier than usual, or perhaps because he'd grown a bit in the year since he'd discovered the hidden platform, one of the wooden rungs—the second to the top—gave way in a violent twist just as his sneaker shoved off it. It spun out of its nail holes and sailed out of sight, landing with a thud somewhere below. With nothing to push his feet against, it took all of Worser's upper-body strength to heave himself, shaking and gasping, onto the rough-planked platform.

There he lay on his stomach, panting, trying to slow the

meteor shower in his head. After a while, his breathing calmed and his mind quieted, leaving only five overriding thoughts. The first was *I'm so very tired*. The second was *I'm stuck up here*. The third was *No one will know where to find me*. Next was the biggest of all: *I've done a terrible, unforgivable thing*, followed closely by *I'm in serious trouble*.

Like a cruel and very limited jukebox, his attention shuffled among those few realizations, until it shunned all but the last two and kept them on repeat. Worser slumped against the tree trunk, feeling, in so many ways, rotten. He thought of nothing else—not even the passage of time.

At some point, when the sun's light struck him sideways through the trees, he heard a noise. A rhythmic crunching of leaves and snapping of twigs told him someone was coming. Worser scooted back from the edge of the platform and tried to be as still and quiet as the rest of the tree. He hoped it was a dangerous fugitive and not anyone he knew and loved.

"Worser?" called out a familiar voice.

He felt a warm, rushing sensation in the center of his chest. Donya was here looking for him—a fact both dreadful and wonderful.

"We're almost there," he heard her say.

"How high up is it?" came another voice. Turk. He was here, too. A fact that was only awful.

"Look there! See it?"

The footfalls came closer.

"Worser," Donya shouted up to him, "please come down."

"I can't."

"Look, I know you're upset about what happened. But hiding won't help."

"Was anyone..." Worser's voice trembled to the point of being unintelligible. He cleared his throat and tried again. "Was anyone hurt?"

"Everyone's fine," she said. "They all got out safely. A lot of us are worried about you."

"I didn't mean to set the store on fire."

"I know."

"It was an accident."

"I know."

"Total lucky breakage, but the storage room came through okay." Turk's voice was sharp and bugle-like, as if he were shouting through cupped hands. "Our equipment smells like an outdoor grill, but basically our stuff is fine."

Worser wasn't comforted to hear this, but he wasn't disappointed either. "And...the bookstore?"

They were silent a few beats. "Don't know yet," Donya said. "We'll know more later."

Worser let out a soft moan. It was going to be a total loss. There was no other possible outcome. Whatever didn't get consumed by fire would have been saturated by water. All that paper. All those words.

He remembered a line in his Masterwork: *The firefighter tried asbestos she could, but she couldn't put out the fire.* At the time, he'd thought it a clever pun. Now it made him cringe.

Donya and Turk started murmuring together—their words too low and indistinct to be overheard.

Worser stretched out on his back and closed his eyes. It occurred to him that no matter where he went, there was no absolute quiet and no absolute stillness. Along with the two interlopers, he could hear the hum of nearby traffic and the chatter of birds. It also felt like the earth below him was turning—which, of course, it was. Turn, turn, turn. Nothing ever stood still.

"Worser?" Donya called out after a couple of minutes. "Do you want us to go get someone? Maybe your aunt?"

"No."

"Mr. Murray?"

"No!"

"Okay, so...what can we do for you?"

"Nothing. I have to stay up here until I figure things out." He considered a moment. "And I can think better if you're quiet."

"All right."

"Are we supposed to just stand here?" he could hear Turk say.

Donya shushed him.

They were silent for a few minutes. Then Donya shouted up, "Hey, Worser? There has to be someone we could get for you. Herbie, maybe? Who do you usually talk to when you're upset?"

"I used to talk with my mom." He swallowed. Then swallowed again. Then realized what was caught in his throat was a sentence. He let it out. "I really miss her."

"I know."

"Wait. But I thought his mom was back at the—"

"*Shhhhhh!*"

"Okay, okay."

"Hey, um, I know I'm not your mom, and I'm certainly not as smart as she is," Donya said. "But maybe you could come down and talk about it with me?"

"I can't."

"Library Boy," Turk called out. "I know you're dismay-hemmed, but if you won't come down, it's harder for us to help you."

"I didn't say that I *won't* come down, I said that I *can't*. One of the top rungs came off when I climbed up, and the next one is too far down for me to reach. I'm stuck."

"Oh."

"Turk, go find help. I'll stay with him."

"Hang tight, LB," Turk called out. "We'll get you down."

Next came tramping noises that faded into the distance.

Worser turned onto his stomach and peered over the edge of the platform. Donya, still in her lemon-colored dress, was sitting against a nearby ash tree.

"You don't have to stay just because you feel sorry for me," he said. "I'll be okay. It's not like I can go anywhere and get in any more trouble."

"Shut up. I'm not here because I feel sorry for you."

"Then why—"

"I'm here because I care about you."

"You do?"

"Of course." She pulled her knees to her chest, yanking down the skirt of her dress. "I was wrong when I called you a stuck-up know-it-all—sorry about that. I know Turk isn't Rhodes Scholar material, but I also think it wasn't fair for you to judge him. I like that he likes me for who I am, so I accept him for who he is, you know? And I accept you, too. I was just angry when I said we weren't friends. I do want to be your friend."

A tiny smile crept onto Worser's face.

Friend. He mouthed it, tasted it. The word was too short for such a big concept. It started off too softly and ended with *end*. It deserved at least three syllables, stronger consonants, and long vowel sounds.

"Anyway, sometimes I lose my temper and let my words get ahead of me," she went on. "No matter what, I'm glad you joined the club."

"I'm not sure the other members will want me around anymore after this. Plus, I yelled at them today about their writing."

"You think I haven't done that? It's, like, the Lit Club way. If anyone's feelings are hurt, they'll shake it off by the next meeting."

"But where will that be?"

"Don't know. We'll figure something out."

Worser was quiet for a moment, ruminating on his possible future. He might not have a place anymore, but he had people. The thought steadied him.

"Is Turk going to join the club?" Worser asked. "I still find his abuse of certain words rather upsetting."

Donya laughed. "He does that on purpose, you know. He's a lot like you."

"How is he like me?"

"He has fun with words. It's not that he doesn't understand them; he just... changes the rules for how they're used. Language evolves, right?"

She was correct. Language, along with everything else, changed over time. There was no way to avoid change. But one could make peace with it.

"You just assumed he didn't know better," Donya went on. "You were judging him. Unfairly. That's why I got so mad."

"Sorry." Worser watched as a breeze lifted strands of Donya's hair and fluttered the sleeves of her dress. "Thanks for staying here with me."

"No problem."

"And thank you for being my friend. I'm your friend, too."

"I know. We've known each other a long time, Worder."

He pushed himself to a sitting position. "Did you just say *Worder*?"

Donya grinned. "Yeah. I've been thinking, and I've decided it suits you better. My uncle Raymond loves birds—loves to see them, take pictures of them, teach people about them. People call him a *birder*. You're that way with words, so... *Worder*."

One of the many curious things about humans is how bold they can be when they feel they have nothing left to lose. Worser couldn't save the bookstore, or Lit Club, or his mom, and he couldn't even begin to imagine how much trouble he was in, so he cared little about saving face.

Thus, it was with very little fear and hesitation that he rose to his feet and called out, "Donya Khoury, you're the most beautiful girl in school—probably the whole town. I would say county, but that might be veering into hyperbole. Even among all the girls in the state, you're likely in the top fifteen percent."

"Uh, wow." Donya chuckled nervously. "Thanks?"

"And, Donya...?" He waited for her to meet his gaze. "When we're older and more responsible—and maybe have our advanced degrees—do you believe that you and I could be more than friends?"

Her eyes widened. "I... don't think so. Sorry."

It was the pause that spoke to him. For the first time, he understood what Aunt Iris meant, back when she was introducing him to her p-ohms, about sometimes having to let things be, and about the spaces between words being full of meaning. Donya's brief silence was a cause for comfort—three dots of an ellipsis, like three seeds of hope.

He smiled down at her and she smiled back. He wanted to stay awhile in that moment—to make it last long enough to become a tangible thing, the way silt hardens into rock or vapor condenses into water. But he couldn't, because there were sirens in the distance, and for the second time in a span of three hours, the local fire department was summoned because of one William Wyatt Orser.

A.k.a. Worder.

The bookstore was still standing. The fire had been quickly contained and put out, but all of the stock was damaged by either smoke or water. In addition to the books, there was one other casualty: Worder's Masterwork. It had gone up in flames with most of the bathroom. Nothing left of it to salvage.

The fact that he'd left it behind—even in a panic—was astonishing. For years it had been with him constantly. Like an extra appendage. Now that it was gone, he couldn't quite feel the loss. It was just one deep current in the river of his emotions.

He wasn't sure how the firefighters who rescued him from the tree house knew he'd been the one who started the bookstore blaze. Maybe Turk had said something when he called for help, or Aunt Iris had, or someone else who'd been at the scene of the fire had mentioned his name. It didn't really matter. It was the truth. He was responsible.

After the firefighters set up a long metal ladder and guided him down, they took him to their fire station, where he was met by Aunt Iris and an arson investigator. The investigator asked him a lot of questions about what had happened at the bookstore, along with questions about his feelings and his home life. She was kind and patient, and Worder answered honestly. When she seemed satisfied that he wasn't a danger to others or himself, she handed him off to his aunt. She told Aunt Iris that she believed that community service would likely be sufficient punishment—but emphasized that it was up to a judge, not her, and she couldn't make any promises.

It was just past dark when he was brought home, shamefaced, fatigued, and draped in a gray blanket that Aunt Iris promised to return to the local unit. Worder stepped from the plant-free porch into the foyer and stopped. He found it difficult to go any farther.

"Oh, Ms. Lucretia, you are a gift from the universe," he heard Aunt Iris say from the living room. "How can I ever thank you?"

"No problem. Constance fell asleep soon after you left and is still asleep," Ms. Lucretia replied. "How about you bake me another batch of those yummy scones and we'll call it even?"

"You have yourself a deal."

Ms. Lucretia came around the corner and halted in front of him. "You've got leaves in your hair, young man."

Worder kept his eyes on the floor tiles. "I've done a terrible thing," he said.

"Hm. Well. What are you going to do about it?"

Worder rummaged through his mind for an answer. "Apologize?"

"That's a start. But that's just words. Actions are more powerful. They show you really care."

Before he could even glance up, Ms. Lucretia opened the door and headed out into the cool, gloomy evening.

For some immeasurable amount of time, Worder remained standing and thinking. Eventually, he wandered into the kitchen, where his aunt was bustling about. In front of his chair, she set a small plate that held half a sandwich and a pickle. He took his seat and began eating. Soon, she sat down across from him, teacup in hand.

For several minutes, they ate and sipped in silence. Worder waited for a scolding, or a graphic account of her arduous day, but there were no words—just the whir and clink of a spoon in her teacup.

Finally, he could stand it no longer. "I'm sorry," he said.

Her mouth curved into a small, sad smile. "Thank you."

"I should be saying thank you to you," he went on. "I see now how much you've been doing for me. And Mom. For a long time."

Aunt Iris's eyes filled with tears. She said nothing—just pursed her lips and nodded.

He took a shaky breath and continued. "I do believe Mom was doing her best after Dad died. But when you're sad or in pain, it's difficult to think properly."

"That's true."

"I understand what she was going through. I mean, I didn't lose Mom, not like she lost Dad, so it's not the same. It's just that she's changed—everything's changed so much."

"It is pretty much the same. Change *is* loss."

Worder stared down at the crumbled remains of his turkey on rye. The image slowly blurred. "Tell me the truth. Things will never go back to the way they were, will they?"

"No. They won't. I'm sorry."

He nodded slowly.

"Of course, I suppose they never do," she added.

Something slid against his leg. Peering beneath the table, he saw that Seer had joined them.

"But everything will be okay." Aunt Iris swiped at some nearby crumbs with her napkin. "We will be fine."

It was a simple declarative sentence with four single-syllable words. And yet, somehow, it was powerful. A strange sense of calm began to seep through him.

Worder slowly turned his plate, thinking. "Did you know that there's no actual future tense in the English language?"

"Oh?"

"We can speak about the future, but the verb doesn't change from its present-tense form. It's only through the use of auxiliary verbs like *will* that we denote future tense. Like *I will go* or *I will be*."

"Fascinating. I wonder why that is?"

"I don't know," he said with a shrug. "That's how it's always been. The only way we can get out of the present and into the future is with help."

After dinner, Worder stepped into his mother's room. He realized that was how he thought of it now, instead of the study. His mind conjured the phrase *Mom's bedroom*. It felt more and more like her, too. There was a jar holding flowers she'd picked on a walk. A bowl filled with pieces of quartz—also found on walks. And now, Worder noticed, two framed pictures on the wall—her finger painting and his daisy painting.

There was also a photo of her and his father, sitting on an unfamiliar couch, holding hands. As he looked at it, he thought about how her life had capsized when he died. How it must have divided her existence into before and after, then and now, familiar and unfamiliar—just like her stroke had done to his.

Quietly and carefully, Worder moved various objects off the nearby chair—her pegboard, a string of beads, her cat-ear headband, a colorful woven poncho—and sat down.

"Hi, Mom," he said.

Her eyes opened. "Be," she whispered. Her smile was tired, but warm. The right side lifting higher than it had weeks before.

"Guess what? I lost my words, too."

Her face radiated understanding and sympathy.

"I'm going to have to start over, the way you are." He gazed down at the back of his hands, which bore a slight scrape from the tree house and somehow a smear of mustard from his sandwich. "But also, I'll have help, like you do."

His mom shifted and reached out her arm, and her right hand landed atop his.

"Mom?" he said, his voice cracking. "I...I love you."

Her hand lifted and aimed toward the photo of him and the bear on the nightstand. "Beh?" She raised both arms and extended them toward him. "Beh?"

It was as if a light came on in his mind. Suddenly, Worder understood.

"Hug? You want a hug?"

She grinned. "Beh!"

That's what she had been gesturing to in the photo. Not the plush toy itself, but his clutching it to him.

Worder stood and leaned into her, letting her arms encircle him. He rested his head on her shoulder and closed his eyes. For the first time in what seemed like forever, everything made sense.

And for the rest of the evening, no one said a word.

TWENTY

Restore

"I suppose you'd like to know why you were called in here, Will," Mr. Ludlum said.

"I assume that I'm being reprimanded for something."

"Actually, no." The principal nervously shuffled papers in front of him. "I heard about what happened last month. With the fire. That was...unfortunate."

Re-Visions, ironically, had become quite popular after its demise. The local daily newspaper was filled with letters to the editor lamenting the loss of the town's only non-university bookstore, and one of the commonly stated arguments was that such a store could instill an appreciation of literature in the youth of the community.

Worder cocked his head. "Are you sure I'm not being reprimanded?"

"No, no," Mr. Ludlum said. "I just wanted to talk to you and—"

A knock on the door interrupted him. "Ah, yes. Here she is now. Come in!"

The door opened, and Donya stepped into the room with a very confused look on her face. Her eyes passed from Worder to Mr. Ludlum and back again. Worder shrugged to indicate he was as bewildered as she was.

"Thank you for coming, Donya. Please sit down."

Slowly, warily, Donya settled into the chair beside Worder's. "What's this—" She caught herself and began again. "May I ask what this is about?"

"I was just about to tell Will that I regret my not supporting the Literary Club earlier this year."

"Okay..." Donya slid her glance sideways toward Worder. He shrugged again.

"It really is a shame that such an organization would be forced off campus," the principal went on. "We need more young people like you to take an interest in writing. I'm afraid it's not possible for me to renegotiate the library hours, but I believe I've come up with an alternate solution now that you've lost your meeting place." Mr. Ludlum paused to take a breath before saying, "I have a key to the library, and I could let your club use it after school once a week. I could also serve as your sponsor, but I wouldn't need to attend the meetings—I'm assuming I can trust you to behave yourselves while I work in my office. I will just need to read anything you decide to publish in your magazine at the end of the year to make sure it is appropriate. And the school will find the funds for it. What do you say?"

Worder looked at Donya. "This is your decision. You're the club leader."

"Maybe we could be co-leaders?" She grinned at him.

There was an ease between them now. He still maintained his nearly lifelong crush on her, and it still hurt to see her hold hands with Turk, but at least he'd earned her friendship. Unlike before, he didn't need an excuse to approach her, talk to her, or invite her over for scones and a writing session. Donya had even joined him a couple of times in reading picture books aloud to his mother—a daily task he'd taken on, to help her associate words with their images.

His relationship with Donya was changing, but it was a change he gladly accepted.

"All right, then," he said, returning her smile. "I think we should take Mr. Ludlum up on his offer."

"I do, too."

"We accept," Worder said, turning toward the principal.

"Good. I look forward to working with you, Donya and Will."

"Mr. Ludlum? Could you please call me Worder?"

The coffee shop was the type his mother, just a year earlier, would have described as *horrendous*. It was designed in that impractical, deconstructed style with exposed pipes and vents and air trunks, a stained concrete floor, and enormous windows—leaving nothing to absorb sounds. The walls and ceiling were painted matte black, and light was provided by spidery metal sconces and strands of white holiday lights draped around poles and window frames. Right inside the entrance stood a driftwood Christmas tree decorated with knitted balls, looking, in Worder's opinion, like an oversized cat toy.

Still, he knew, he should order something. "A cup of Earl Grey, please," he said, choosing one of the familiar items on the menu board. While waiting for the barista, Worder noticed a row of sugar-crusted chocolate-chip muffins in the display case in front of him. "And one of these, please," he added. "To go." Herbie would love it. He could give it to him when he went to his house later that day to watch old episodes of *Doctor Who*. Holding his cup and saucer in one hand and the muffin bag in the other, he walked carefully to a nearby table.

Worder felt odd sitting there—misplaced. But he felt slightly awkward everywhere lately. On his way in, he'd caught sight of his reflection in the glass. The pants he was wearing, one of the pairs his aunt had bought for him, were now ending at his ankle bones. His limbs appeared to be elongating. And only two days before, in the bathroom mirror at home, he'd glimpsed a bony protuberance in the center of his neck. Transformations had been happening all around him, and now they were happening within him. He was a stranger in his own body. A changeling.

His discomfort intensified as soon as he saw the familiar shape trudging into the coffee shop. Faded blazer. Wild, penguin-crest eyebrows. Battered paperback clutched in his right hand. Unlike Worder, Mr. Murray appeared to be unchanged. Worder knew he shouldn't find this surprising, as it hadn't been that long since they'd last seen each other. And yet so much had happened that it felt as if years had passed instead of weeks.

As Worder's thoughts went back to the fire, a minor version of that day's panic took hold. His vision swirled slightly. His knees jiggled beneath the table. And his right palm squeezed his left fingers, as if he were trying to hold his own hand.

Mr. Murray nodded in greeting, ordered coffee (in a to-go cup, Worder noted), and sat down in the vinyl-and-chrome chair across from him. Worder studied him closely, looking for any signs of animosity. But the man seemed cramped and uncomfortable more than anything. And there was something altered about him after all—his side hair stuck out more than usual, obscuring the view behind him. He was all Worder could see.

"Thank you for coming," Worder said. His voice was high and breathless, devoid of all power.

Mr. Murray again nodded, then busied himself with adding sugar to his coffee, avoiding Worder's gaze.

After about half a minute of quiet between them—amid the reverberating racket of the coffee shop—Worder took a deep breath and made himself say what he had come to say. "I'm sorry."

The man nodded yet again and stared down into his cup. "Yeah."

Worder wanted to collapse across the table and beg forgiveness. Instead, he repeated, "I'm sorry."

"Don't get me wrong, kid. I was mad as hell. Not just mad—scared. I'm still a little scared, to tell you the truth. But I'm not angry now. Not any more than usual."

"My counselor says that anger is how some people deal with fear."

At the mention of counselor, Mr. Murray's eyebrows rose half an inch. Worder still wasn't used to admitting it, having been to only a few sessions so far. But according to the giant wall calendar, he'd be going for at least several more months. He would, as his counselor, Sarah, liked to say, acclimate.

"Your being mad was understandable," Worder continued. "I even wondered if you might sue me for destroying your livelihood."

Mr. Murray grunted. "Do I look like a shakedown artist? Everyone knows it wasn't on purpose. But you're lucky, kid. Insurance could have gone after you or your family and made things even worse for you guys. This was a big deal."

"I know. If it makes you feel better, I've started doing my community service."

"Oh yeah?"

Worder nodded. "I help sort things at a thrift store that raises money for charity. I'm actually quite good at it. Clearing out your storage room was excellent preparation."

"Huh," Mr. Murray said. "How about that."

Silence again settled over the table—becoming more unbearable by the second. Worder shifted uneasily. "I'm sorry I hurt you," he said. He realized he had now apologized three times, but it didn't feel redundant. On the contrary, it felt as if he couldn't apologize enough.

"Yeah, well. I'll be okay," Mr. Murray said. "Maybe even better than okay. Maybe this whole ordeal taught me a thing or two."

"Like what?"

For a long moment, Mr. Murray sat and gazed into the distance, as if watching his thoughts on a faraway screen. "Look," he said eventually. "It's like human history. We were apes, and then we changed and became annoying humans. Some change happened slowly, but a lot of it happened fast—because it had to. The food those folks ate died off or migrated away, so they had to move, too—or find new food. They had to adapt. It was lousy times, I'm sure, but it led to some positive results in the long run. Do you see what I'm saying?"

Worder considered lying but decided not to. "No."

"Eh, sheesh. What I mean is, there at the store, I was stuck. Floundering. And the fire? Well, awful as it was, maybe it was the kick in the pants that'll help me evolve."

"But what will you do now?"

"I don't know. Hopefully, something that doesn't involve

working with the public. I've had my fill lately. Yeesh, people are aggravating."

"And unreliable. Sometimes ruinous."

Mr. Murray smiled his almost-smile—brows up, eyes wide, the folds of his face smoothing a bit. "Yeah, well, I've been talking to your friend's dad. Dr. Khoury? He set me up with an opening at the university. Library work. Archives. It could be...less aggravating. For a while, at least. Ultimately, I want to become my own boss again at something. That works best for me."

"Maybe this will help." Worder pulled a rectangular piece of paper from his back pocket and slid it across the table.

"What's this?" Mr. Murray unfolded the cashier's check and read it. His eyes opened wider than Worder had ever seen them. "Ah, kid, no. I don't want your family's money. I know you've been going through hard times."

"It's *my* money. I've been saving it." He felt no need to mention that Aunt Iris, with her new power of attorney, had seconded his idea and cosigned the check.

"This much? That's impressive, kid."

"And I want you to have it."

Mr. Murray shook his head. "It was a freak thing that happened—I get that. Insurance already compensated the owner of the plaza. And, remember, I was going to close up shop and get rid of the books anyway. So I don't need your money. Besides"—he gestured at Worder—"you're just a kid."

"I never did like you calling me that."

"Right. Sorry, kid."

"I think you should open a new bookstore."

Mr. Murray rubbed his hand over his whiskers.

"And since I was the one who ruined Re-Visions, I'm the

one who should help you replace it. It's only right. It's logical. Besides"—Worder poked absently at the bag that held Herbie's muffin—"the town could use a bookstore. *I* could use a bookstore."

Mr. Murray propped his forehead in his left hand. "I don't know."

"This time around you could do things differently—like hire people to handle customers, so you don't have to deal with the annoying public."

"If only."

"But I could still come by to see you. Like before."

Mr. Murray sighed. It was a long, slow exhalation—as if he were letting go of something inside him. Afterward, he tilted his head, focused on the black expanse above him, and began to nod. "So, if this were to happen," he said to Worder, "would we rebuild it the way it was? Or would we make it different?"

"It's up to you."

"Nope. It's up to *us*. If you give me this much money, and your family approves, you'd be a part owner in the business."

Worder's mind whirled. "You would trust me? After all that happened?"

Mr. Murray shrugged. "I figure you'll be less likely to burn the place down if you own a stake in it." Catching sight of Worder's stricken face, he added, "I'm only half-serious. Trust would take time."

"Undoubtedly. But I'll make it up to you. I promise."

"Also, building a business involves crazy amounts of work. Think you'd be up for that?"

Worder sat up straighter. "I could handle it."

"Good." Mr. Murray took a sip of his coffee. As he set the

cup back down, he glanced across the table and met Worder's eyes. "I got used to seeing you, kid. It felt weird not having you around."

"I missed you, too."

Mr. Murray made a sound. It took Worder a second to realize it was a laugh.

"You know what, kid? You seem different. You've changed somehow."

Worder grinned. "Good."

Acknowledgments

I want to thank Worser for staying in my head for so many years while I worked on other things, and I want to thank my steadfast agent, Erin Murphy, and my extraordinary editor, Margaret Ferguson, for believing in this quirky kid and helping to make his story so much better.

I am indebted to the following people for lending their expertise: Collette Haney, MS, CCC-SLP; Ralph Castillo, FPE; Dr. Robert Ginsberg, MD; Jeanne A. Trombly, MS, CCC-SLP; Josh Erickson of American Family Insurance; and Louise McDermott, MA, LPC.

Huge thanks to supercopyeditor Janet Renard, wonderproofreader Hayley Jozwiak, and the fabulous team at Holiday House who helped turn my coffee-stained and tear-stained manuscript pages into an actual book: Michelle Montague, Terry Borzumato-Greenberg, Sara DiSalvo, Darby Guinn, Drew Seeger, and Kerry Martin. A special shout-out to Sarah J. Coleman for somehow plucking my mental image of Worser from my brain and recreating it in her brilliant cover art.

I am fortunate to be part of several writing communities. Thank you to my friends at the Erin Murphy Literary Agency, the Writers' League of Texas, the Austin chapter of the Society of Children's Book Writers and Illustrators, and the Vermont College of Fine Arts Writing for Children and Young Adults program for listening to early snippets of this draft and encouraging me to keep going. Thanks also to Owen Egerton, who invited me to read at his One Page Salon back when *Worser* was literally only one page long. Extra thanks to Mike Guentzel, PMP, for being my technical advisor as well as a good friend.

The following people helped me track down information, connected me with key sources, answered questions, shared insight, and/or listened patiently as I grappled with ideas: Esther Ford, Jim Ford, Julie Carolan, Sean Petrie, Siân Rees Haney, Pat Zietlow Miller, Clare Dunkle, Kari Anne Holt, Cynthia Leitich Smith, Liz Garton Scanlon, and Varsha Bajaj.

To my children: Thank you for being so understanding when I am distant and distracted. To Ernie: Thank you for the nuzzles and much-needed walks.

And last but never least, thanks to my alpha beta reader, foolproof proofreader, head cheerleader, and love of my life, Chris Barton. For better and for Worser, I'm so glad we're married.